I0708202

TIM MILLER

NINE OVER PAR

GP

GNATCATCHER PRESS

Nine Over Par
Copyright © **2023 Tim Miller**
All rights reserved.
Print Edition
Published by **Gnatcatcher Press 2023**
San Marcos, CA, USA

No parts of this publication may be reproduced, stored in a retrieval system, or transmitted in any form or by any means, electronic, mechanical, photocopying, recording, or otherwise, without the prior written permission of the copyright owner.

This book is sold subject to the condition that it shall not, by way of trade or otherwise, be lent, resold, hired out, or otherwise circulated without the publisher's prior consent in any form of binding or cover other than that in which it is published and without a similar condition including this condition being imposed on the subsequent purchaser. Under no circumstances may any part of this book be photocopied for resale.

Ben, I realize now that nothing I can write here is going to change your behavior. The fact that you continue to put my books inside "sandies" (as you call sandwiches), in blatant violation of US copyright law, makes me feel sad, frustrated, and worried. Yet I've made my peace. Ben. I have two things to say, if you're still reading: 1) It is my opinion that you need professional help. Talk to someone before you end up in jail. 2) Do you have to use so much mayonnaise?

Cover design by Jessica Bell
Interior design by Amie McCracken

ALSO BY TIM MILLER:

Spooves
Reading Ketchup
Phickshun
Nine Under Par

TABLE OF CONTENTS

WARM-UP SWINGS

Metropolis Writers Workshop
Online Stand-Up Comedy Course Level B
Assignment #1
Gene Santos

June 14th, 2017

So I think I stumbled on a pretty amazing new theory the other day. Like AMAZING NO ONE HAS EVER PUT IT TOGETHER BEFORE amazing. I've been going over it in my head and I'm thinking it's pretty airtight. So give it a listen and you tell me if it's genius. Prrrrrrreetty sure it is.

I think that the difference between men and women, in terms of appetites, is exactly the same for both SEX and ... MEXICAN FOOD.

Think about it. Men will eat Mexican food anywhere, anytime, and whenever possible. Women? They have to be in the mood.

Men have no problem eating Mexican food twice in one day. Who do you think invented the breakfast burrito?

For men, both the quantity *and* the quality of the Mexican food establishment has a relationship with the amount of drinks they have consumed. Have you been to a taco stand on a college campus at three a.m. lately? Not a pretty sight.

And yes, when you add booze to the mix, there are some disturbing implications concerning the male sex drive. But let's focus on the ones who hit the Taco Bell drive-thru at two in the morning and then spend an hour in the bathroom the next day. I mean I've seen cats turn down Taco Bell meat.

Men don't care about the cleanliness of a Mexican food establishment. For the most part, the dirtier the restaurant, the better the food.

Men will eat Mexican food that they know they shouldn't. That leftover burrito they found in the fridge, not exactly sure how long it's been there, doesn't smell quite right? Ah, what the hell!

Women prefer high-quality Mexican food, food with a future. A dependable restaurant that you can take kids to. They like it clean, with impeccable service.

Sure, there are your outliers out there. There are women that love Mexican food and will eat it 24/7. And there are men that don't like it at all. Strange though; I've never met one. But they're out there, like UFOs. They have to exist, these outliers, just like UFOs have to. You know there's just too much space, too much probability, and somewhere there has got to be something.

Nope, I've never met a man that doesn't like Mexican food, and I can't imagine I ever will. Literally I can't imagine a grown man ordering a hamburger at a Mexican restaurant. Or being out with a bunch of dudes eating fish tacos and being like, Ew, gross. I hate tacos. Literally never been said by a male. It's like trying to picture life 100 years from now—it's just beyond the scope of my imagination.

Telling you. Pretty sure it's airtight. Men and women. Mexican food and sex. Ex. Act. Ly. The. Same. Try it out. Do a little experiment: See if you can get your wife or girlfriend to either have sex with you or get Mexican food when she's not in the mood. Not gonna happen.

INSTRUCTOR FEEDBACK:
Great material here, Gene! You had me laughing out loud—harder to do on the page than the stage :) Really nice opening and flow

throughout. There's good buildup in the introduction and I can feel the timing as I read. You've made some nice connections between two separate topics that everyone has some knowledge of—Mexican food and male/female sex drives.

As you develop this material, see if you can work in more specific, authentic examples from your own life. A girl you dated, someone you know, maybe even your current significant other. Maybe you can specifically address an outlier or an anomaly, and therefore share in the surprise with your audience. Also, by being specific about a person, it steers your material away from the Stereotype Wasteland (see reading for next week!).

Remember, the more the audience knows you and can relate, the more they will laugh. You've got a great start here. Now, apply the lesson from this week's reading and see if you can take the laughter from general and really hone in on the specific.

-Rob

A SMALL BUCKET

Mike hit his six iron, a slight pull, and sang along to the Steely Dan tune in his head, the one he listened to on the way over to Encinitas Ranch. He saw Gene coming from the parking lot.

"What up, Mike?" Gene said, approaching the range.

"What up?"

"Here we are."

"Amazing."

"Really doing it."

"Someone's got to."

"Golfing on a Wednesday."

"Golfing on a Wednesday."

"So good."

"Not complaining."

"Definitely not."

"Aren't you a little early?"

"Huh?"

"You know," Mike said. "You're not, like, running up to the 1st tee with the starter calling out your name with your shoes untied while you text your wife."

"Oh, right. Yeah. I'm just going to hit this bucket and then I have to run an errand before teeing off. That way I can still follow my pre-round rush-up-to-the-tee routine."

Mike poured out some balls from his bucket on the ground in front of Gene and resumed both hitting and humming the Steely Dan tune. He was about twenty balls in, working the mid-irons. They had the middle of the driving range to themselves. The right third of the range had a youth girls' clinic going on.

"So no Dave today?" Mike asked.

Gene started to stretch, using an iron to loosen up his shoulders and back. "Nope. Guess he's doing another show in San Fran. The life of a stand-up comedian is unpredictable. It's like being a doctor. You're always on call."

"I guess my golf game will have to provide the comic relief," Mike said.

"Yours and mine both—vast and fertile comedic ground."

Gene began to swing a warm-up tool that consisted of a heavy rubber ball on a flexible shaft, the idea being that, if the shaft flexes too much, something's off with the tempo of the swing. Gene's swing didn't necessarily accrue this benefit, and he more or less treated this part of his warm-up the way an on-deck batter in baseball treats a bat with donut weights.

There were a few golfers smattered along the semi-oval range, including an Australian scratch golfer they had played with a week ago.

"Did you see our friend?" Gene asked.

"Yeah," Mike said. "He was here before me. No wonder he's so good—he practices."

"Bet he'd be pissed if he has to play with us again."

"Right. He'd be like, These two yutzes?"

Gene was done swinging and began to hit balls, starting as he always did with his pitching wedge before working his way up through his lofted irons. A friend had recently shown him how pros hit balls on grass tees—the club making a row of divots, moving balls into the next grassy space, and proceeding efficiently and methodically like a typewriter. Gene's space was already pretty choppy, and he struggled with this facet too.

"Did you see the Yankees signed Chapman?" Mike asked.

"Yep. It was a good ride while it lasted."

"I'll say. I may have to trade him now, just on principle," Mike said. "I cannot have a Yankee on my fantasy team."

"That and the whole choking his wife thing," Gene added.

"As a fantasy sports manager," Mike replied, "I pride myself on my high fantasy ethics."

"Plus, you'll get a lot for him. Dude's a stud."

"Beast."

"Are you still alive in football?"

"No, I lost my first-round playoff matchup. But I have a shot in my pick 'em league. I'm in fourth place and only a few points behind third. The top three place."

"Nice. You should probably pick against the Bears this Monday."

"You're probably right."

They hit in silence for a while.

Mike was hitting his driver. Gene had moved up to his seven iron. Around them, Southern California's winter sun poked through the clouds, looking like a lukewarm biscuit. The surrounding hills and ridges loomed like mirages of ships in the distance. To the west, the ocean beamed winter's solid dark blue. The voices of the coaches running the clinic could be heard over the steady and irregular thwaps of the amateur golfers. From beyond the hills to the north, a low *boom* reverberated from Camp Pendleton.

"I believe there's a potential snare for our get-together for the game on Monday. The wives have book club."

"Yeah, you're right," Mike said. "Though I think it's now just a wine club. Carla, Mitch's wife, can't seem to remember not to host on Mondays. You'd think she'd be able to plan around the NFL, which only has games on Sundays, Mondays, Thursdays, and Saturdays in December. Sheesh." He was finishing his bucket with a few wedge shots. Gene was now hitting his rescue club.

Gene laughed. "Speaking of which," he said, "did you hear what happened to Carla's sister Morgan?"

"No. What happened?"

"I guess she was walking home from the Christmas party last Saturday—the one Michelle went to alone because I wasn't going to be the only husband there—and Morgan ended up in the hospital and had to have emergency brain surgery."

"What?"

"Yeah, I guess Morgan's neighbors called about a break-in, so the cops came by to her neighbor's place at three in the morning. They didn't find any thief, but they found her lying on the ground a few steps in front of her door with her head split open."

"Shit. Is she all right?"

"They think she's going to be OK. She's still in the hospital but should recover. She has a shaved head."

"Do they know what happened to her?" Mike asked. He was done now and began washing his clubs. When he dunked them in the club washer they made low *splunk* sounds. When he brushed them dry, it was with high-pitched, crisp scratches.

"There's no sign of foul play. There's the fact that the neighbor called about a break-in. The thinking is that the robber tried unsuccessfully to break in and bumped into Morgan. But Morgan is a pretty big drinker. Michelle said she was drinking but didn't seem any drunker than usual. Michelle also left the party before Morgan, so maybe she could have drank more. But Michelle said that apparently no one saw her leave and the thinking is she just up and walked home from the party. Alone. Not the best neighborhood for that, over by the beach with all the transients."

"Is there any kind of investigation ongoing?"

"Nope. The cops are just calling it a drunken fall."

"Damn. Shit's crazy."

The starter made an announcement.

"We're on deck," Mike said. "Better hit some putts."

"Couldn't hurt."

They walked toward the cart Mike had already reserved, looking ahead to the round in front of them with that blind optimism golfers always carry to the 1st tee. The Steely Dan song, still on a loop inside Mike's brain, rose to the surface and he let it out, singing high and clear in a falsetto voice, loud enough to make the Australian scratch golfer look up.

NO. 1
TRAVIS

I haven't been playing much. Besides a couple of rounds with Gene at Encinitas Ranch over the holidays, I've basically been on a hiatus. The last six, seven weeks have been nothing but kids and work and dishes and the house.

So I joined the Lomas Santa Fe Executive Players Club. Twenty-five dollars a month for unlimited golf. I figure I can play on the way to work and get out at least twice a week. Last Friday I got out after work. It was my wife's idea.

"You need to," she had said. "Get outside, relax. Blow off some steam."

I have been a bit of a grump lately. The grind. I own my business, putting musicians on cruise ships. I'm lucky to be me. It's great, beyond fortunate. But it's nonstop, and that can wear you down.

She practically made the tee time for me. Lomas Santa Fe Executive is a chill place with a relaxed vibe. On the 7th hole there's a view that looks over the Five, out across Solana Beach and down to the sea. I like to stand there and breathe. When the wind is out of the west, you can taste a hint of salt in the air.

I called up Gene and he said sure, he'd be down. But then his kid got sick, so it was just me.

It was a perfect San Diego spring day. Bright sunshine. A little on the cool side, but not bad. Maybe sixty-five degrees. I ended up getting paired with two singles: one old guy and one young. And they each drove a cart.

The young guy's name was Travis. He was maybe twenty-four or twenty-five. Said he only started a year ago and that he's playing four or five times a week, all right here at Lomas. A graduate of Torrey Pines. Doing cabinets for his dad. Kind of an odd character. Long hair. Mustache. Tucks his ears into his hat, like most San Diegans, which I've never quite understood. And his clubs' headcovers were random. One was Barney Rubble from *The Flintstones*. One was Chewbacca from *Star Wars*. The third was a bat. Said he found them all right here at Lomas.

"Turned 'em in and when no one claimed 'em after a week, they were mine."

I was a little skeptical that he'd bothered to turn them in. Also his phone ring was Rodney Dangerfield's horn from *Caddyshack*. I thought it was an ice cream truck in the valley the first time I heard it. He seemed to enjoy the confusion he caused between me and the old guy. I lost track of how many times his phone rang on the front nine, but at least four of them were during my backswing. Finally on hole number 8 he answered a call.

"No, I can't," he said. "I'm still at the Escondido job." I looked over at me and winked. He was that kind of strange, that he would wink at someone he hardly knew.

The old guy was named Harold. After introducing himself, he said, "If you young fellers wouldn't mind, keep an eye out for my ball. I don't see 'em much anymore. Which has its advantages."

I thought he might have a sense of humor and that by the 3rd hole we'd be calling him Harry, but that's about all he said on the whole front nine. Harold had those dark, thick old-man sunglasses and moved pretty slow. Probably north of eighty. He had a full head of bright silver hair, with thin, hairless, white old-man legs and the requisite geezer gut. Still getting around, though. But barely.

The front nine was pleasant, despite Travis's phone ringing every other hole and the fact that he was smoking cigarettes. My mind needed a break from work visas and flight schedules and cruise dates. Instead of my computer screen, it was nature and sunlight and fresh air. Travis wasn't exactly helping, but what can you do?

Then, on number 10, it happened. If you've never played Lomas, it's another 90-yard hole, uphill, with power lines running across it. Funny, all the times I've played Lomas, I've never hit those power lines. But I've seen it plenty.

Maybe that was a sign, because I got up there and hit my sand wedge flush, and wouldn't you know it instead of nice high trajectory right at the pin, my ball struck the power line smack in the center, sending it on a sharp ricochet that flew off and bounced down the road. I remember the power line made an odd, low, warped sound, like some giant had snapped a long metallic whip.

So then Harold got up there, and his ball sailed right through the lines, landing just short of the green, as all his shots did.

In my mind Harry smiled and said, "Guess we won't need to call the power company on account of me," but Harold just stepped on his divot and didn't utter a word.

Then Travis was up, and he winked at me again. He was grinning, and I couldn't figure out why. Peculiar as that Barney headcover. When he swung, though, I understood right away.

It was like a gunshot. A loud boom that likely reverberated all the way down to the ocean.

"That was loud," Travis said, looking around as if he didn't know what caused it, like with his cell phone.

I watched as the grin on his face vanished faster than you could say "heart attack."

I turned and Harold was on the ground, clutching his chest. When I looked back over my shoulder, Travis was taking off. I heard the tires on his cart squeal as he stepped on it and drove away.

I went over to Harold. He lay clutching his chest, and a little white foam started trickling out of his mouth. I lifted up his sunglasses and he looked up at me with wide, light blue eyes. I held his stare while I dialed 911. I didn't dare look away, like between our eyes was a lifeline, a supernatural power line keeping him in our world. But I could see he was nearly gone. I told the responder on the phone where we were, then I whispered to him. "It's gonna be OK. Keep breathing."

I thought I saw something in his eyes, a flicker. Maybe sadness or even anger. He tried to speak then, but it was just a gurgle through the foam.

"The ambulance is on its way," I said. I opened his mouth and tried to think back to my last CPR training, fifteen years ago when I sang on a cruise ship and it was mandatory for all employees.

Then he died, on a perfect Friday evening in March, on number 10 at Lomas, the road hole under the power lines.

The ambulance arrived in about ten minutes, just as the group that had been far behind us—an Asian woman and a young girl who I presumed to be her daughter—came up to the tee on number 9. I saw the woman looking down the hill at the ambulance. Her daughter was no more than eight or nine years old, so they just bypassed it all and walked over to 11.

The paramedics took Harold away on a stretcher. When I told them what happened, they called in a police officer and instructed me to meet him at the clubhouse. They offered me a ride, but I said if it was all right with them I'd just as soon walk. So they took my contact information and we shook hands. That's when one of the paramedics, a young guy, found the wrapper. It was a firework. A pretty hefty explosive called a Bacon Snap, illegal in California but easy to find on the black market or any fireworks stand in states where they're legal.

The sun was going down by then and it was cooling off. I figured this would catch up with young Travis, since they probably have his credit card and address and such. All the ducks that normally hang out on the pond behind the green on the 4th hole—another 90-yard par 3, this one uphill—flew over my head as I walked along. I looked up at the mallards flying off, the setting sun making their bellies glow, and thought, Now there's no doubt in my mind. No way that kid waited around a week for someone to claim that Barney Rubble headcover.

NO. 2
THE LINKS LIGHTER
PART ONE:
TWO GOLFERS

"It hurts my heart, Pete."
— William Faulkner, *Two Soldiers*

October 30th, 2017

"Hear my voice and say *shhhhhhh* …" Gene said in his teacher voice.

An Indian girl was the only *shh*. No one was listening.

He shouted, "One, two, three. Eyes on me!"

"One, two. Eyes on you!" half the class parroted back.

"Let's settle in sixth graders," he said. "We have a special class today in honor of Halloween tomorrow." He moved about the room, putting out small fires of conversation, while a group of students passed out the science notebooks. For him, every school day had an element of Halloween. The affable Mr. Santos, STEM science teacher, was like a costume he wore Monday through Friday.

Three boys whispering and giggling in the corner represented a stubborn holdout. Gene cleared his throat and stared at them. On the table next to him was a flashlight, a pink rubber model of the human brain, a plastic mini skeleton affixed to a thin metal rod, and one of his golf clubs, a four iron.

"Before our activity," Gene said, grabbing the flashlight as he moved back toward the door, "to wrap up our unit on the nervous system, I would like to tell you a story. A true story." He hit the light switch. The room went dark, the only light coming from a bubbling red volcano in the fish tank in the back of the room. He leaped forward like an actor from the wings of a stage, twisting his back to the audience. He spun around, clicked on his flashlight, and held it below his chin.

"The story of Phineas Gage."

A girl screamed, with mirth and not fear. Silence hung in the air as the fish tank bubbled.

"Before I tell the story, please open your journal, write today's date, October 30th, 2017, and title your page 'Mr. S's Halloween Tale of Horror.'"

The class complied. Gene listened to the sound of scratching pens and pencils. This was the part of teaching he loved—when it felt like performing. He held the flashlight up like a police officer, casting it down on the open notebooks.

"Halfway through the story, I will pause and ask a question. After the story is over, please write your takeaway, any connection you can make to our learning about the brain. When you're ready to listen, put your pen or pencil inside your journal, close it, and look at me."

He held the flashlight under his chin and waited. They all obeyed, for once.

*

"Phineas Gage was a railroad worker in Vermont," Gene began. "A foreman in charge of blasting rock in the 1840s. He was a good worker. Everyone liked him. To clear rock for the tracks, he would place dynamite into a small hole, sprinkle some sand over it, and tamp it down with a long rod called a tamping iron." He demonstrated by dropping imaginary dynamite, sprinkling invisible sand, and tamping it down with the grip of his four iron. "One day, just as he turned his head to say something to the men behind him—possibly a joke of some kind—the tamping iron hit some rock, caused a spark, and the dynamite went off accidentally right by his feet."

Again, silence—a rarity for this group—amid the faint bubbling of the fish tank.

"The tamping iron, 1.25 inches in diameter and three feet, seven inches long, surged right through his skull." In slow motion, Mr. Santos guided the four iron toward his own face. "The iron entered his cheek bone, went behind his eye, and came out the top of his head."

"Yikes," a boy with braces said.

"Yikes is right," Gene said, using his index finger to nonverbally remind the boy to refrain from comments, a clear expectation during a Mr. S story. He now took up the pink rubber brain, pulling it apart and holding up the left hemisphere. "Like a javelin, the iron went through the left side of his frontal lobe before exiting the skull, sailing through the air, and landing some eighty feet away. Eight. Zero. They found the rod smeared with his brains and blood."

Gene held out the rubber model and, with sleight of hand, the iron appeared to penetrate the squishy pink sulci. With elaborate care, he set the model brain down and carried the golf club in an arc across the room. The students' heads all followed the trajectory.

"And then …" Gene held the light right up to his face and leaned down at one of the more talkative students, whom he could see was legitimately apprehensive. "Phineas Gage got up and walked away."

Gene let the surprise linger. He moved about from table to table, feeling the eyes of the room watching him. "He survived. Yet poor Phineas, from this point on, would be known as neuroscience's most famous patient. He walked to the nearest oxcart and got a ride back to his lodgings. A doctor visited him that night and treated his wounds. Here I will pause and ask my question. Knowing what we've learned about the various functions of the different lobes of the brain, please open your journal and write down any limitations Mr. Gage might have had after his accident."

Gene flashed his light from table to table, reading as the students recorded answers. Once a majority had finished, he continued. "The physician, a man by the name of Doc Harlow, had a limited knowledge of head injuries from horse kicks and gunshot victims. Still, he cleaned and dressed the wound. It would be another twenty years or so before Pasteur published his theory of germs and diseases, so Harlow didn't really understand what he was up against. Still, he went to battle against the danger of infection, not only germs but also fungus, as evidenced by a mushroom that flowered from Phineas's skull. To the doctor's amazement, over the next few weeks, Phineas recovered.

As many of you have correctly stated in your answers, the damage was not to the reptilian brain, the area responsible for vital functions like heart rate and breathing. The damage was to the front of his brain, the area responsible for decision-making, personality." Gene couldn't help himself. "You know, the part that's not fully formed in adolescent brains—the part that considers consequences." He scanned the room, slowing his gaze on the mischievous members of the class.

"What happened to him?" asked a blonde girl with glasses.

"Well, the story gets a little fuzzy from there. Remember, this was the 1840s. There was no internet or television or even radio. Scientists didn't know what part of the brain did what. The story of Phineas Gage is a remarkable story of human survival and a turning point in our understanding of neuroscience. In many ways, he became a mythical figure. The railroad refused to hire him back. He toured for a time in a traveling show, you know, for 'freaks.' He tried to work. But no one knows for sure what he was really like. There were no blogs or Instagram posts. The details of his daily life went unrecorded.

"Some scientists used his story to support their claims of phrenology, which was a pseudoscience based on the sizes and shapes of heads. One phrenologist went so far as to claim that the top of the brain was closest to heaven and therefore appealed to people's better angels … and the bottom, lower part of the brain, is vulnerable to the

Devil's fires from down below." Gene flashed his light at the volcano in the fish tank. A nervous giggle filled the room.

"Some of these pseudoscientists claimed Phineas became a drunk and a lout. That he was no longer a good worker or even a good person. That he stopped working and became a vagabond, wandering from place to place. All hearsay. There's no real evidence that any of that is true. The real story is that Phineas made a substantial recovery. He had problems. Memory, fatigue, perhaps depression, stuff we would expect from a severe injury to the frontal lobe. He worked at a stable in New Hampshire for a time. He made his way down to Chile and worked as a stagecoach driver for a period before he came home and went off to work on a farm in California. All the other stuff about his personality is basically exaggerated and unsubstantiated."

Gene returned to the middle of the classroom. He felt like he was standing center stage, putting the finishing touches on a monologue in a Broadway play. He held out the golf club, like a symbol of Misfortune. He aimed his flashlight at the golf club's blade and continued in a solemn tone. "He carried the tamping iron around with him the rest of his life, sort of like a companion. He lived twelve more years before he had a bout of seizures and died on the West Coast."

Gene observed the faces under his spell. He felt triumphant.

"The doctors remembered him and wondered about him, so after he died in San Francisco, they asked his family to exhume his body and bring his skull all the way back east. Now his skull and tamping iron, along with this photo, are on display at Harvard Medical School."

Timing it perfectly, Gene flipped on the lights and turned on the projector, revealing two pictures: one of the grinning, cracked skull of Phineas Gage from Harvard Medical School, and the second, a black-and-white daguerreotype of Phineas in a suit and tie, young and handsome but for one closed eye, posing with his tamping iron.

"Now, please write down your takeaway, and then we have enough time for a brief hands-on activity. When you finish writing, put your notebook away and get a paper template to make some crawly spiders. Thank you for being a good audience."

"We love it when you tell stories," a student said.

Gene replaced the golf club, flashlight, and brain. His elation subsiding, he walked around the room as the students wrote and drew. He paused over a girl with her hair dyed bright pink. Ellie was a sensitive, artsy type, and she was sketching a portrait of Phineas Gage. All the drawings in her notebook were vivid, graphic, and full of detail. He looked over her shoulder as she penciled in the scar, then she guided the tip of the pencil over the mournful expression and etched a tear. He took two steps away from her desk and stopped. Backtracked. Something wasn't right.

Instead of Phineas Gage, the mournful expression was his own.

*

Gene stood on the edge of the crowded putting green and tucked in his shirt. All around him golfers putted, chatted, and laughed in the bright evening sunshine. An announcement came over the clubhouse loudspeakers.

"Good evening, and welcome to the final night of the Twin Oaks Monday Night Golf League. Thank you for a fantastic season. Tonight's format: Partner Best Ball, three holes from the red tees, three from the white, three from the blue. Please make your way to your carts in the next fifteen minutes, where you'll find your assigned hole for tonight's shotgun start. And most importantly, remember to have fun."

Gene stepped onto the putting surface. He rolled his first three practice putts at a nearby hole, all of which went straight in. His phone buzzed in his pocket. It was Dave.

Be there in 5

He retrieved the golf balls and, bending over in his putting stance, felt constricted by his tucked-in shirt. So he untucked. His next three putts missed. The loose shirt was interfering with his backstroke. He scanned the other men putting and classified them into two groups—the tuckers and the untuckers. He felt like he fit in more with the tuckers.

A tucked-in shirt says something about a person, he thought. That they have all their ducks in a row. So he retucked.

He resumed putting, and his thoughts became like fingers picking at knots. To tuck or not to tuck was on the surface of his consciousness. He reached down and found a superficial bothersome truth: the form letter-style rejection email he received this morning from a prominent satirical internet website. He'd submitted a spoof about his Saturday morning writers' group—with what he considered deft use of each writer's idiosyncrasies—in which they legitimately endeavor to critique a death threat to Chicago Bears quarterback Jay Cutler.

Gene's putting was erratic as his mind dug into how tonight he would open the Google Drive folder labeled "Humor Writing" and update the spreadsheet labeled "Submissions" containing six years' worth of rejections (and one acceptance, from a blog that was now defunct).

Below this was a murky layer from which floated buoyant and slippery knots. They popped up like whack-a-mole. His anxiety for the future. Vague knots of uneasiness. Getting older knots. A small, tight knot for dying.

Then, deeper still, all the old knots, the frayed unpickable ones, the regrets and indecisions and disappointments and guilt, deep down in the brain, surrounding the Big Knot—that he was a coward, that his life was a lie and a failure.

Fuck it, he thought, and untucked his shirt. He examined the grip of his putter. Rather than replace the grip when it needed it, he had used some white tennis tape he'd found in the garage. It worked for a time, but now the grip was dirty and loose. One more thing he had neglected to do right.

He adjusted the loose tennis tape, removed his visor, and ran his hand through his short, thick bristle of dark hair, recently speckled with gray on the sides. The sound was not unlike an iron through thick grass. He replaced his visor, took a deep breath, and hummed a few tuneless bars. Like flipping a switch, he left his knotted thoughts alone and instead focused on the physical laws necessary to swing a metal blade to knock a plastic and rubber ball into a hole in the ground.

"There he is," Dave said, walking toward Gene. Dave dropped three brand new gleaming white golf balls that hit the surface with little pattering thuds.

"In the flesh," Gene responded without looking up from his practice putt, which curled in. The men, friends since childhood, bumped fists and started rolling in four-footers. They were about to complete their sixth year playing together in the Monday night league.

Dave lined up his putt. He was short, Black, and muscle-bound from excessive weight training. It was these muscles, concentrated primarily in the upper body, along with his stage antics and facial expressions, that sometimes drew comparisons to Kevin Hart. Even though to Gene, they didn't look that much alike at all—besides the muscles.

Dave farted a little squeaker of a toot. He acted like he accidentally squirted a little spray of poo in an imaginary golfer's line. He pretended to apologize and then asked the imaginary golfer if he wanted the squirt of poo moved over to the left or right. Gene, as often happened when Dave got going, was left speechless.

Dave marked the imaginary poo with an imaginary ball marker, got a final confirmation, and decided the joke was over. "So what's new?" he asked Gene.

"I recently attended a training for the Next Generation Science Standards."

"That's hot."

"The standards are three-dimensional."

"Yowza. I could listen to you talk about those things for days."

The cup full, Gene dumped out the balls. They sorted them and Dave resumed putting. Gene pulled a Sharpie out of his pocket and began writing a message to himself on his slightly used ball.

"What's this week's message?" Dave asked.

"Today I'm drawing inspiration from a maxim inscribed on the Temple of Apollo in ancient Greece," Gene said.

Dave returned a blank stare.

"Know thyself."

He held up the message he had written to himself three times, one on each ball: *U Suck.* "I can write it on yours, if you want."

"As a rule, I don't let anyone write on my balls," Dave said.

Gene corralled his three and scooted back. "Have it your way," he said. He did a few practice swings, experimenting with his backstroke and the untucked shirt.

Like Gene, Dave moved back and resumed putting. "So you know Bob McLauren?" Dave asked. "Opens for my Comedy Showcase thing at the Store."

"Sure. Has the real manic act," Gene said.

"That's right, the McManiac," Dave said. "And you saw him on a night when he didn't have his usual Monster Energy cocktail."

"So?"

"Before last night's show, he fell off his bike on the way to the gig."

"Is he all right?"

"He wasn't wearing a helmet."

Gene emptied the cup and sorted. He started fiddling with his shirt, folding the front into something like a semi-tuck.

"I guess he didn't want helmet head for his show," Dave said. "Anyway, it was a freak thing. Some kid pulled out of the alley right in front of him. Bob went over the hood of the kid's car and landed on his head."

Gene whistled and did more practice strokes.

"From what he remembers, he lost consciousness for a minute or so. But he came to and actually got back on his bike. He made it just in time for his act."

"And how did that go?" Gene asked without looking up. The semi-tuck had come loose and was brushing up against the tennis tape.

"Not good. He kept losing his train of thought. It turned into a slurred ramble about his headache, the bright lights, being dizzy."

Dave paused. "The crowd wasn't very sympathetic. One patron thought he was drunk, and that's when things went south."

"Uh-oh." Gene abandoned the semi-tuck experiment.

"Bobby started rolling around on the ground, as if he was on fire."

"Like he was burning?" Gene asked.

"Right. A hallucination. He thought he was burning alive. It freaked out the audience. Everyone assumed he was on drugs. They had to call an ambulance. The whole thing. The place cleared out. People got refunds."

Gene left a putt short and Dave knocked it back to him. They each moved back to practice ten-footers.

Gene tried a side tuck, which appeared to work because he rolled in back-to-back putts. Dave filled him in on the visit to the hospital, and how Bob remained convinced that he was covered in third-degree burns.

"How is he now?" Gene asked.

"I got a call from Rich at the Store this afternoon," Dave said. "He no longer thinks he has burns, but they're still running tests."

"I guess that's a good sign."

"Rich asked me if I knew anyone that could fill in for a couple months."

Gene's putt lipped out.

"What?"

"I need someone to fill in for Bob. To open up for the Sunday Showcase at the Store. Someone not named Jacob Cohen."

"No thanks." Gene said. A new knot formed in his mind.

"C'mon. Twice a month. Two months tops, four shows."

"Nah."

Gene moved back to putt from fifteen feet. His thoughts groped down for the old knots, but it was like he couldn't find them, just when he needed them.

"C'mon, Genie. I need a favor. The young comedians in the show-case need a favor. It's terrible following Jacob's 'Nobody Loves Me' act. You've seen it. Plus, it will be like the old times."

"That was improv," Gene said. "Not stand-up." Gene left a putt woefully short, then rolled the next one way past. "And it was almost twenty years ago."

"Didn't you tell me that over the summer you took an online class in stand-up comedy?"

"So what?"

"What was the point if you're not going to say it in front of a live audience?"

"Not interested. I've got kids. Bedtime routine. My teaching job in the morning. That class was a waste of time. I just needed a distraction from tantrums. I never even finished it. I can't be out at crazy hours in La Jolla doing stand-up." He found the Big Knot.

"Jesus," Dave said. "Listen to yourself. It's not like I'm asking you to do *Saturday Night Live*. It starts at seven. You'll be home by ten."

Gene steered two of his golf balls toward the one that had sailed past. He turned away from Dave to aim at a different hole that already had two golfers putting at it. His mind was picking, picking. Dave left his balls in the way of a recently arrived golfer and stood in front of Gene, blocking his putt.

"What is it? Are you afraid you'll fail? Or are you afraid you'll succeed?"

"I'm not afraid, Dave. I just don't have the time. Two words: three kids." Gene rotated away from his friend's obstruction and instead aimed a lag putt at the edge of the green. The Big Knot felt good. He wasn't picking it so much as rubbing it.

Gene smacked the next two without stopping his putter.

"I'm going to ignore the complicated math in your last statement. Jim Gaffigan has five kids. Look at it as material. Your story about Ally and the light switch? Or Lucy and the water? Dude, that would kill."

"I'm not doing it." Gene walked off. Dave followed him.

The clubhouse speaker cackled, "Carts away."

"Can we just drop it?" Gene scooped up his balls and walked with all the other players toward the line of carts. Dave trotted over to retrieve his balls and chased after him.

"All right, what about this?" Dave said, catching him at the edge of the putting green. "In addition to the league best ball, we'll play our own private match. Straight up. In the unlikely event that I win, you open for me at the Showcase."

Gene sighed and made a face. "You're not going to let this go, are you?"

"It's a ten-minute set. It's cake. A walk in the park. A walk in a cake park."

Gene looked away and then back at the face of his lifelong friend, the scrawny kid that once got teased for being too skinny, now Dave Love, a semifamous stand-up comedian with an oversized upper body. But he still had toothpick legs.

"All right. I'll tell you what. I'll take the bet. One, just so you shut the hell up about it. And two, if I win, you have to contribute to my blog."

"Your blog?"

"Yeah. The Humor Faucet."

"I didn't know you were still doing that."

"Oh, come on. I've asked you a dozen times to write for it. You always say sure, but you never do."

"The Humor Faucet."

"That's right," Gene said. "Keeping the humor flowing."

"Does anyone read it?"

"Not really. Mostly confused plumbers. But there is one guy in Alaska who thinks it's hilarious."

"All right. It's a bet. Do the jokes have to be about faucets?"

"No, man. It's a metaphor."

Dave winced and shifted into a slow, greasy Southern drawl. "I heard a guy on TV talkin' fancy once."

"Don't worry about it. Let's play."

"Mmm, mmm, mmm, I like dem faucets dat have hawt *and* col' wat-eh."

"Would you c'mon?"

Gene tucked in his shirt.

"Oh shit, he's going tuck, ladies and gentlemen," Dave announced. They made it to their cart.

"How was your show in Houston last week?" Gene asked, pulling out some tees from his golf bag and putting them in his pocket.

"It turns out two months is a little soon for most people to laugh after a catastrophic hurricane," Dave responded.

"Things still pretty bad?"

"It's a mess." Dave nodded, grabbing two beers from the cooler. "And using curse words as hurricane names didn't exactly slay."

"Bummer."

"Hurricane Asshole. Hurricane Bitch. Hurricane Cocksucker. I thought it was good material." Dave shrugged. "I also tried hurricanes with baby-talk names. Hurricane Ootsy Wootsy has been lowered to a category 4. Hurricane Cuddle Wuddles will make landfall on Tuesday. Crickets."

Gene and Dave sat down in their cart near the end of the long line of golf carts leaving the clubhouse, a slow and merry train. The shotgun start had them teeing off the 3rd hole first, so they had a short ride ahead of them. Gene put his beer into his koozie. They cracked their cans open, cheersed, and pulled away. As they drove along the 1st hole, Gene caught sight of a red-tailed hawk swooping down and quickly rising skyward, something small and brown in its talons.

Death is just a hawk in the sky, he thought. He found the small, tight knot and gave it a few scratches.

The evening was cloudless with a warm breeze. The cart train cruised along with two foursomes and four carts breaking off at each hole.

"How was class today?" Dave asked.

Gene recapped the story of Phineas Gage as they drove at the one speed allowed by golf carts—slow. They arrived at the 3rd tee, but they were the second foursome to tee off. They waited back while the group in front of them hit away. *Thwack! Nice ball.*

"Anyway," Gene continued in a hushed tone so as not to disturb the second hitter. "All of that stuff about him being a louse is basically exaggerated and unsubstantiated—just part of the legend and myth because he did, for a time, do some exhibition stuff."

Dave nodded. "I identify with touring freaks."

Gene took a sip. *Thwack! That'll play.*

They were out of the cart and swinging now. They introduced themselves and greeted their playing partners: two short, stocky, mustached brothers, John and Jerry. The sun had started to fade and the grass glowed luminous in the twilight.

They selected a white tee for the 175-yard par 3. Gene bent down to tee up his ball.

"Looks like Christmas came a little early this year," Dave said.

Gene smiled and hit it flush onto the center of the green.

Despite the stakes of the match, they started out like always: coming up just short of caring very much about a white ball rolling into a hole. They made fun of each other, they made fun of golf, and they made fun of each other making fun of each other. They couldn't tell John and Jerry apart, and they made fun of that.

*

On both the 3rd and 4th greens, with Dave already in for bogey, Gene missed makeable par putts of around six feet. On their third hole, the par 5 5th, Dave made an up-and-down sandy par from an awkward stance in a bunker to go 1-up.

"Well done, sir," Gene said, retucking the part of his shirt that had come loose. They curved around toward 6, a short par 4, and stood waiting. Dave took a call on his cell. Gene opened his third beer and waded out into his thoughts. He thought back to the artsy girl's drawing of his face as Phineas Gage.

Alcohol had an interesting effect on the knots in Gene's mind. They dissolved, vanishing like salt crystals in a class experiment. They were still there, and similar to most of his fifth graders regarding charged particles, Gene was none the wiser. On the phone, Dave slipped in and out of an Australian accent. Gene hummed, watched butterflies, and sipped his beer. He closed his eyes and listened as Dave finished up a conversation with his manager.

The cart girl drove by. Dave made a joke about ordering whole milk.

"Two percent? Skim? But that's my final offer."

The girl drove off laughing. The milk reference triggered a memory for Gene. He thought back to high school, to the first time the Love family invited him over for dinner. Being with Dave and his twin brother Eddie was a comedic experience, with each brother trying to one-up the other. They challenged each other, with one taking big gulps of milk while the other tried to make the gulper laugh, doing whatever it took for the gratifying white spray. Halfway through the meal, the table was dripping with milk.

On the 6th hole, both Dave and Gene drove tee shots into the fairway. They waited for John or Jerry.

"Ah, holy hell!" John or Jerry shouted after pulling his drive into the bushes. Dave made a face at Gene.

The milk-soaked dinner was right after Gene's parents had divorced. The Love brothers were adopted as babies by white parents outside of Nashville Tennessee. Their family bounced around for the first twelve years of life before arriving in Gene's hometown of Riverview, Illinois, in time for the twins to start high school, which also happened to be the week Gene's parents' divorce was final.

It felt like a sitcom, like they had been brought to Riverview specifically so that they could meet Gene. Like it was Fate that brought the three of them together. As things got rougher between his splintered family, Gene spent more and more dinners with the Loves. He used to daydream that the Love family would adopt him.

The practice of spitting milk drove Mrs. Love crazy, considering how extremely skinny both the Love children were. She wanted to make every calorie count. But Mr. Love couldn't help but chuckle.

"Roy, you're encouraging them," Mrs. Love would say.

It was after the fourth or fifth dinner that Gene learned the true root and genesis of the humor for the twins, the very source and beginning of it all: sitting around watching *The Three Stooges* with their adopted father.

John or Jerry hit his second ball into the bushes. "God dammit! Whore bag!" he shouted. He walked back to the cart, red-faced, picked up another ball, and hit one short and to the right. "It's going to be up to you on this hole," he said to his brother.

"At least it's in play," Jerry or John said. "C'mon."

"Excuse my French, fellas," John or Jerry said in a gravelly voice to Gene and Dave, walking back to the cart. Then to his brother, "How do ya like that? Goin' along, just fine, then out of nowhere. Like my brain clean forgot how to hit a golf ball."

The brothers drove off. "God dammit! Whore bag!" Dave said with uncanny precision of inflection and tone. The two friends drove up and hit from the fairway. Dave went long into another greenside bunker. Gene pushed his approach shot just off the green. Back in the cart, Dave started talking to Gene about his new sand wedge, but Gene wasn't listening. He had opened beer number four.

Gene's thoughts reached for one of his favorite old knots: the memory of him and the Love brothers as teenagers. The three of them had dreamed of doing comedy together, inspired by the great stand-up comedians and humor writers of television and movies in the late '80s and early '90s.

"It's actually a 57 degree," Dave was saying. "It's heavy as shit. I use it for curls."

Gene went over to his ball and almost chipped in for a birdie. He walked up and tapped it in, picking up his ball and rolling it around in his hand. How he loved this knot, this memory of the three of them. It was soothing for his mind to nibble and chew on it. It helped him fall asleep at night. After college, in their tentative Y2K-early-20s-life-path-forging, both Dave and Gene enrolled in the Last Laugh improv school in Chicago, following in the footsteps of so many of their heroes.

"You guys are fucking funny dudes," their instructor said to them after one performance. "Careful. Or you'll end up famous." His voice still echoed in Gene's ears.

After a few years of steady advancement in the classes you had to pay for, Gene and Dave both took the opportunity to transfer to the West Coast when the Last Laugh opened a school in LA. They were offered positions teaching a couple nights a week and performing with a new comedy troupe, the Ouch! Potatoes.

Dave blasted out of the greenside bunker to within a few feet of the hole, but the subsequent putt rimmed out.

"Sorry, Dave. No gimmies. Otherwise I woulda given that to you," Gene said. The match was all square.

Dave became Lloyd Christmas from *Dumb and Dumber*. "Oh, no, Mary, I couldn't possibly accept that. Not after all we've been through."

Gene laughed.

Dave put his putter away. "How about a hug?" he asked.

Gene saw John or Jerry make a *can you believe these guys?* face at Jerry or John.

"Here, have some chips," Gene said, back in the cart.

Dave accepted, adopting a slow, low-pitched, depressed tone. "I eat when I'm sad. And I'm sad when I eat."

Gene took a sip, and began eating chips too. On the course, both he and Dave played mediocre bogey-train golf for the next hole, but Gene wasn't really there for most of it (which might explain the bogey). He was back with the Ouch! Potatoes, riding high on a wave of strong reviews from their first season. But then Life got in the way. The group had trouble staying together, generating material, and gelling with new members during the second and third seasons. It was after the third season that their roads forked.

After the 7th hole, Gene finished his beer and stepped into a porta-potty. Just a fork in the road, he thought. After the Ouch! Potatoes, Gene fell into his job teaching science at an elementary school. He had just enough college science credits from his General Studies BA to qualify for a specialist role at a charter school, conducting experiments; the school hired him while he worked on his credential in night school.

Standing in front of kids wasn't that far off from improv—just different hours and different subject matter. Like in improv, he learned the hard way, on his feet with rough days. But the night school classes were a cinch, and that's where he met his wife. They each had two licenses stamped in the same summer: one for marriage and one for teaching.

"Gene, you OK in there?" Dave shouted from the tee box. "Are you going number two? Is it 'rhea? Grunt once if it's 'rhea?"

Gene stepped out of the porta-potty. "Just fine; thanks for your concern."

"Phew, he's OK, folks!" Dave announced, clapping. "Porta-potties are scary. They can change your life. I have a friend, went into a porta-potty, was never the same."

"Oh yeah?" John or Jerry said.

"OK, it was me. I was a tall white dude before a porta-potty at Encinitas Ranch."

Both John and Jerry laughed.

Dave gave Gene a look. Like, See, I knew I could crack these nuts.

They each opened another beer as they waited on the 8th tee box, another short par 4. Two quick bogeys and they stood waiting on 9, a par 4 along the driving range with water and a picturesque fountain near the green. (Like life, golf rounds always seemed to slip past too quickly to Gene.) Dave was talking to John and Jerry about their industrial plumbing business. They had not heard of the Humor Faucet blog.

Gene sat in the cart and noticed the rising moon. And now with beer number five, a cluster of old knots rose to the surface. Sadness and Regret and Guilt latched together into an especially intricate knot—his marriage.

It was an old song. The fire had gone out. She didn't understand. She never really did. He didn't know how to say it. Then the first kid came along and it was too late. The automatic sidewalk was moving and there was no getting off. Next came the second and then the third kid, and suddenly comedy seemed like the moon, far away but always peeking over his shoulder.

Gene listened to Dave ask questions about industrial plumbing. Dave literally can talk to anyone, he thought. He had become a fairly successful stand-up comedian—digging for laughs in the territory just beyond most people's comfort zones. The stage was like an extension of the dinner table with his brother Eddie; he wanted the audience to laugh so hard and so suddenly that they sprayed their drinks. He could do spot-on impressions, voices, and accents. Scottish, Australian, and American Southern were particularly in his wheelhouse. Celebrities, movie lines, cartoon characters, Siri, Alexa—he had a Swiss Army knife with endless blades of voices he could use to penetrate people's defenses and carve up laughs. Whenever he felt an audience slipping, he could always pull out an accent or voice and yank them right back.

Eventually they each teed off. "Good ball." "Nice one." "Beauty." But then Dave sliced it badly into the bushes along the 8th hole fairway.

"C'mon, guys, no one's gonna say anything about mine?" Dave asked with mock petulance.

"We're speechless," one of the brothers said.

Dave quickly made a name in the LA scene and then started traveling to San Diego and Palm Springs. He found himself with offers to join other touring comedians around the country. He flew out on Thursday, did shows Friday and Saturday, and flew home Sunday. Twice a month, he hosted the Comedy Showcase at the Comedy Store in La Jolla on Sunday nights. Monday he golfed. Tuesday he wrote more jokes. He made a good living.

"You know what I really appreciate about you, Gene?" Dave said as the two poked around the bushes with their clubs.

Gene shrugged.

"That you always help me find my balls," Dave said. "It's important in life to have someone to help you find your balls."

"Here it is," Gene said. "Titleist 2?"

"See what I mean?"

"What are friends for?"

Since Dave wasn't doing many shows in LA anymore and was sick of the traffic, he moved to San Diego. He and Gene picked up where they left off, making fun of each other and playing in the Twin Oaks Monday Night Golf League. That was six years ago, right when Gene, unbeknownst to anyone, embarked on a career as a humor writer.

On the green, Gene three-putted but still won the hole to go 1-up.

*

They were coming around to their final hole, number 2, a long, tight par 5. The sun had started to fade along the horizon, peeking through and smearing low clouds into brilliant shades of yellow, orange, and purple. They could hear the distant sound of dogs barking and maternal voices calling kids to dinner. Gene swiped his visor across his short, bristly hair, making that sound of a club through grass, and put the visor in the basket of the cart. The setting sun felt good on his face.

All match long, Gene couldn't make a putt to save his life. A self-fulfilling prophecy, the *U Suck* taunted him all round, skimming right past the edge. As a result of his atrocious putting, including four-putting the 5th hole, the match was again all square.

"Isn't it a crime we get to do this while people out there are trapped in offices and traffic jams?" John or Jerry said. They had become downright social.

"Amen, brother," Dave said, raising his beer.

Gene bent over to tee up his ball.

"And I thought today was gonna suck," Dave said loudly, indicating Gene's rear end.

The brothers laughed.

"What happens if we tie?" Gene asked Dave. The brothers knew about the side bet.

"Sudden death on the putting green," Dave said. "We fight to the death, *Game of Thrones* style."

"I'm picturing a gallery golf-clapping after I bash your head in," Gene said.

"Bash my head? C'mon, son. I'm gonna murder your ass with my seven iron. Maybe a six. I'm in between clubs."

Gene pulled his drive and winced as it rattled around in some trees. Next, Dave overswung and wickedly sliced his ball beyond the trees and into an opposing fairway. "At least I'm consistent," he said.

"FORE!" John or Jerry yelled impressively. "You can never be too sure," he added.

Dave drove up to the start of the fairway, and Gene raised his hand with pseudo-seriousness.

"This is where we part," Gene said. He downed what was left of his last beer then grabbed his hybrid, six iron, wedge, and putter. He walked off saying, "No pressure. See you at the green."

"You sure you got everything?" Dave called after him. "There's still a couple clubs in the bag."

"I just like to be ready for the unexpected." Gene smiled over his shoulder.

"Well, if you get hungry, eat something," Dave said, pulling away.

Gene walked along. The final sip of beer passed some critical reaction point, releasing some invisible force. The biochemistry in his brain pressed all the knots on him like a crown of thorns. They were all there, ripe for the picking: all the small insignificant ones, like the grip on his putter, right there with the big ones, like his marriage, his disappointments, and his fears.

God, how he was just so fucking sick of them. But he picked away all the same. He would go home. The two-year-old would be crying in her crib. His wife would be on her phone. "You're up," she would say. And that would be the only words they would exchange all day. And he would go and lie on the floor until the crying stopped.

He thought about how different Dave's path in life had been— though sometimes he wondered, Who got the fairway? There was that, plus the feeling that, teaching science, he was always walking around in shoes that didn't quite fit him. He needed to make people laugh. It was a part of him, and he was only doing it in small, personal ways. He thought maybe, just maybe, he had the talent to make many, many people laugh—a big splash—if he could just find his voice, the one he lost somewhere, somehow, like a set of keys misplaced.

He put his extra clubs down. The next knot he didn't so much pick at as hold up and examine in the evening light. It was a wonder and a marvel: the substance and source of the regret and the need and the giant maybe. All the stress-dailygrind-traffic-parentingsmallchildren-dishes-sleepdeprivation, how it broke him down and made him mope.

"You've got to snap out of this," he heard his wife say. "It's like you're going through life sleepwalking. I don't like it." It was then that he would think of Dave in some distant city, standing in the spotlight, the darkness alive with laughing faces.

John or Jerry hit from the fairway.

Though who knows? Maybe Dave's life is no picnic, he thought in the shade, waiting to hit. Maybe life on the road gets lonely. He had talked to Dave about it some, but he didn't really know how Dave felt. Maybe the sex life, with different women and in different cities, maybe that got sort of old and was actually lonely too.

He did little practice swings, the club wisping through the grass. He found a knot that was well worn, smooth and pleasant to touch: People come into your life and you are together for a time, and then you are apart. And sometimes when you are together you are really together. Like the phrase *cart golf.* Sometimes you play alongside each other, hitting it together and to the same spots, spending most of the round together and talking. Other times you are together with people but not really together, like this hole. You are hitting to the opposite sides of the fairway and just meeting on the green, and there isn't much conversation. Sometimes you go through periods of life when you don't really get to know the people you're playing with.

And the special people go and are gone and are not part of your life for years at a time. You have periods with parents and family and random people and friends and coworkers and neighbors and they are the people in your life and it's always changing. People die and become ghosts in your memory and dreams.

There was some delay on the green and Gene kept waiting, waggling his club. Impatience rose with his belch. What the fuck was going on up there? He tried for another pleasant, smooth knot, but the next one he found was tangled, sticky.

He was lucky. He knew that. Most of his life he had had good people and good family and abundant friends. Yet beyond these rounds with Dave, he didn't have many people that made him laugh like the Ouch! Potatoes laughed, deep down in the gut, just rehearsing, clowning around, eating pizza, living on jokes as much as food. They had studied comedy like medical students studied the body, deeply and thoroughly and around the clock.

He hacked out of the woods with a low six iron that struck a tree flush and came back at him. He threw a *what can you do?* look at John or Jerry.

And now he cupped this fragile, tender and newborn knot: the bet. Maybe the laughter would return? Life was unpredictable, like the kick of a golf ball. Maybe life was one long series of kicks; throughout your days there are approaches where the ball could go either way— fairway or rough, green or sand trap. Sometimes you hit it down the middle and it lands in a divot. Sometimes you hit in the trees and get a kick into the fairway. It's fickle and goes either way: plugged into a lip or caromed onto the green and resting near the Big Flag: Love. And everyone has the tense moments when the future is up in the air, hanging in the balance.

The second time, he had a clear opening. But he lifted his head, hit behind the ball, and chunked it. He fixed the divot by stepping on it, traded his six iron for the hybrid, walked ten feet, and, without his usual practice swing, punched it down the left side.

Who decides? The Fates or God or maybe just an indifferent, arbitrary universe. All you can do is play the ball where it lay, take the good with the bad, the pleasure with the pain, and have hope that the next kick will go your way. And if it doesn't, that's Life.

He needed about a five iron to get the ball to the green.

He didn't feel like yelling over to Dave for a different club, so he just hit it up short with his six iron. He grabbed his clubs, walked forward a few paces, and saw that Dave was still in the other fairway, waiting on the group playing that hole. John or Jerry was searching for his ball in the bushes. Gene stood in the middle of the fairway in the last light of the day. He closed his eyes and figured that he could still get a double with an up-and-down.

He flubbed his chip and was still short. He groaned. Dave's approach landed on the middle of the green.

Screw it. So I'll do some stand-up. It's no big deal. I'll do the shows and that will be that …

Gene untucked his shirt. Dave drove around a hill on the right.

"Fancy seeing you here," Gene said, replacing clubs in his bag and keeping his putter.

"I just figured I'd do something crazy and aim for the actual green."

"Very strategic," Gene said. He skulled his chip across the green. "I think you've got an opening act."

With his hand as a gun, Dave made a gesture like Shooter McGavin in *Happy Gilmore* and drove on around the green. John or Jerry chipped from the rough to just a couple of inches away.

"Good one," Dave called out.

The other brother was in a bunker. He hit with the loud, clean *thump* of a well-executed bunker shot. This thump came moments before the other sound, also a thump but not the deep, clean metal-on-sand sound. It was a horrible, low, hollow sound. A sound that, the moment you hear it, you know what it is. It is similar to the sound of a melon being struck but not breaking, or the cringeworthy sound of an infant smacking their head on pavement. A sound that stays with you, that you remember.

It was the sound of a golf ball striking Gene Santos on the front of his head.

Then there was the sound of Gene crumpling to the ground, so that there were three sounds in quick succession: *Thump. Thump. Thud.*

Moments later, very softly, there was the near simultaneous sound of golf balls landing—the sand shot right near the hole, and the intruding ball coming to rest where the other brother was standing.

This brother, standing near Gene, had flinched when he heard the whizzing sound of the ball descending like a missile. He quickly ducked and stood with one knee on the ground, as if another ball was impending. Dave, thinking about it later, remarked to himself that it was the calm, swift move of an individual accustomed to artillery.

From the back of the green, Dave saw it all very clearly and would continue seeing it the rest of his life. Gene had been across from him, facing the green with his back to the fairway, the setting sun threaded a golden outline on his shoulders. When John or Jerry made the clean *thump* sound, Gene turned to speak, probably to say something like "nice out" because Dave, hearing it later, would always hear a faint "nnniiii" sound just before the second *thump*. Then Gene crumpled and there was the sound of him falling, the body and then the head milliseconds later face-planting on the firm green. Almost like two thuds. Almost.

Dave then looked beyond to see the foursome that had teed off behind them, roughly 300 yards away. He recognized them from the league as the third group to have started on 3, and thought how they would also be trying to finish this hole before sunset. For a moment he was frozen, stunned, alternating his focus between Gene lying flat on his stomach and the group just standing and looking as if analyzing the damage. The moment ended and he rushed over to Gene, rolled him over, and brushed away a few blades of grass smeared on his face. An angry red lump the size of a golf ball pushed through the crown of his head, as if the ball were inside his skin and not on the ground. Below the lump, his eyes were closed and his lids flickered. The word "lolling" came to Dave's mind as he glimpsed Gene's eyes. He would also remember how the tongue slithered thickly around in his mouth. Gene began to moan softly.

The brother near the offending ball kicked it off into the bushes. Dave looked from Gene's face to the foursome out in the fairway, now some 250 yards away. He suddenly felt a strange bond and surge of companionship with these two brothers that he hardly knew, like he could depend on them if it came down to hand-to-hand combat.

"Genie, c'mon, wake up buddy," Dave said. He leaned his head down to Gene's chest and heard the heart beating. It was slow and faint. Gene's chest rose weakly. There wasn't a breath so much as a wheeze.

The brothers stood tensely just beyond Dave and Gene. The offending group stayed out in the fairway watching, assessing. More moments passed. Still, they did not approach.

Gene roused and struggled to open his eyes. Finally, the foursome drove up to the green.

"I was 300 yards away," a man shouted, the cart still in motion. "It was a once-in-a-lifetime miracle shot. One in a million. I've never hit a ball that far in my life."

"Haven't you heard of yelling 'fore'?" Dave asked.

"I just can't believe I hit it this far," the man said. "Never in my dreams did I think I could."

Dave directed half of his attention at the foursome that had just arrived—this short man with a visor and lots of product in his spiky hair, which gave him the look of a hedgehog or porcupine. Dave had never trusted men that used a lot of hair product, and this seemed to confirm his lifetime grudge. Around the spiky perpetrator were three silent faces straight out of a bullying textbook. Dave could see it with a glance at their expressions: They had seen what had happened, knew it was wrong, yet, despite this, they somehow chose to stay loyal to their clan. The other half of Dave's focus glanced down at the stuttering and stirring Gene who began mumbling about how he always knew there would be one more "Big Chance." The phrase kept coming up, surrounded by a random and inaudible slurred babble. "Knoshled burterwise, globla by knowing stungled letex, a big chance, big, wakpuh chance."

The cumulative effect was that Dave wasn't effective at the role of either caretaker or victim's aggressor.

Dave looked helplessly at the two brothers who seemed intent on staying just on the edge of the conflict, ready to spring to action but not about to initiate it. The idea of punching the visored hedgehog in the face flashed in his mind. Dave studied the group of men and did a quick calculus. The two brothers looked like they might know their way around a fistfight, but Dave had never been in a fight in his life and they would be outnumbered four to three.

"Just amazing, caught it flush, maybe a little downwind," the man said. "A 300-yard three wood. Unbelievable."

"I still haven't heard an apology!" was all Dave could finally stammer. The outburst came across as impotent and signaled to the group that there would be no violence, no threat. The brothers relaxed. The man in the visor started over toward the ball that had been kicked into the bushes.

"C'mon, Genie, wake up." Dave lightly tapped the side of Gene's face. One of the brothers helped lift him, and they each put an arm around their shoulders. They carried him to the cart as he continued to mumble incoherently. "We're going to get you to a hospital," Dave said, picking up his phone.

"Just ain't right," one brother said to the other as they went back to tap in their putts.

As they were pulling away, Dave drove with Gene leaning on him like a child; Dave heard the visored hedgehog's voice one last time.

"I figure I can drop it right over by the fringe. Whaddya think, Pete, about here?"

As Dave drove along, Gene nodded in and out of sleep. Dave remembered hearing somewhere that sleep was bad after a concussion, so he lightly tapped Gene's face and called his name to keep him awake. At a turn, Gene's body went limp and he almost fell out of the cart. Dave reached over just in time and pulled Gene back, his head hitting the side of the cart.

"But you were never married, Phineas," Gene said.

In the parking lot, Dave grabbed a bottle of water from his car and splashed Gene's face. Gene's eyes flashed open and the two men stared at each other.

"The knots," Gene said. "They're gone."
"Knots? What are you talking about?"

NO. 3
SO THE RANGER IS
AN AXE MURDERER

On a Tuesday morning in the middle of summer at the Lomas Santa Fe Executive, the ranger pulled up silently to the 8th tee while Mike addressed his shot. Dave nodded and smiled.

Mike hit his nine iron flush.

"Long," Dave said.

"What did you have for distance?" Mike asked.

"About 125."

"Damn," Mike said, looking around the tee in disbelief while making yardage calculations in his head. "I thought it was 140. I can't believe I didn't notice that the tees were up."

"Right swing, wrong club," Dave said and shrugged.

Mike glanced over at the ranger, sitting in a golf cart with an orange flag dangling out the back. She was a small white-haired lady in her early seventies. In the seat next to her, standing on its head, was a bright red axe. She balanced it with her hand on the wooden handle, like a stick shift of an automobile.

"Do you have to put that thing to use when play gets slow?" Dave said with a smile.

"No, it hasn't been too busy today," she said with a completely straight face.

Dave nodded. "Well, OK, enjoy this beautiful evening!"

She waved and drove off.

They started toward the green. Mike was still mad about his shot. Dave turned to him and said, "But when it gets slow, watch out, heads start rolling."

NO. 4
A LOST WEDGE

Gene often thought how his life might have been different if he had stayed with comedy longer. Who knows? Or maybe if the original Ouch! Potatoes could have stayed together longer. They were funny as hell that first season. Fearless. Irreverent. Young. With just the right amount of disregard for society's norms.

The laughter was steady, consistent—an elixir, a potent drug for all that ails. They all got addicted and then they scrambled like addicts when the drug ran low.

Christine, sharp-tongued, tall, and blond, was the natural beauty of the group. She had a natural feel for the sweet spot of man's desire, in between the forlorn and the ludicrous, the dirty and the clean, the wholesome and the lascivious. She knew how to come right up to the edge but then let the audience's imagination, always superior, deliver the goods. She radiated beauty, confidence, and fun. She was the hot girl that was your friend and drove you crazy.

She left after the first season for a pilot opportunity in New York with a complete sleazebag. It stunned the group. Everyone saw it was transparent and flimsy, but no one could say it directly—except Dave, with all the tact of a bulldozer, which just pissed her off. Then she was gone, just like that. The pilot fizzled, and a friend of a friend relayed that she had become another pinball bouncing around in the New York actress/comedy scene.

Then there was the forty-five-year-old Puerto Rican, Helmer, the oldest of the group who looked sixty-five but acted twenty-five. Gay and proud and secure in himself, he spoke and thought a mile a minute and loved everything always. He had a heart the size of an ocean and the mouth and bilingual vocabulary to share it. He was perpetually hurling Puerto Rican expressions and slang that everyone and no one understood. He could exchange witty repartee with a pole. Loud and impulsive, one minute he was a mature and wise philosopher, the next a petulant child, and then a strange amalgamation of the two. He left right after opening night of season two to return to San Juan to take care of his sick mother. That night he was like a firecracker, exploding with emotion and joy, but then fading into a profound, somber melancholy that never goes far in improv. He could only muster sighs for the last hour of his final show and was too emotional to say goodbye.

Tiffany, Black, maternal and sweet, but with a healthy dose of don't-play-with-me that gave all her jokes a delightfully nasty edge. For all intents and purposes, she also left during season two. She had to take on a second job when her ex stopped paying child support, so she was often absent during rehearsals and shows, or she would show up unexpectedly and throw everyone off.

They went from ten members in season one to seven and a half when season two began. The directors filled the two open spots with funny people from the improv school, but the chemistry had changed. Frank took Helmer's spot. He was a boisterous wise guy with slick hair and a slick mustache. He slayed in class with his brutal honesty but clammed up on stage in front of a live audience. He couldn't deliver when it counted.

Jessica, a tall, dark-haired beauty selected to fill Christine's shoes, wanted it too badly—certain death in comedy. She didn't have Christine's knack for holding off and staying quiet, knowing when to back off and let a scene be real and awkward and funny. She had to say something to try and make it funnier, but it always had the reverse effect.

And then the real blow to the Ouch! Potatoes was Billy's out-of-control drinking and drug use. He had it. He was a star waiting to be discovered. It was natural to him—the timing and feel. He seemed to have an infinite supply of material. He also had experience, good looks, and, maybe most important, a genuine ability to make all people laugh. He was funny as hell, and even Dave had to concede that the title of "funniest" belonged to Billy.

He also had manic episodes, demons, and an addictive personality. The addiction was in his DNA. His father was a drunk that abandoned the family when Billy was six. He had grown up with an abusive stepfather, a big-time pitcher that blew out his elbow and became a minor league baseball announcer that took out his frustrations about career and life on his stepson. Billy grew up in the desert under the shade provided by the dugout of the Lancaster Jethawks. It's where he learned to joke around and be one of the guys, watching the players intently with big, sad, brown eyes. He loved baseball but didn't have the talent to play even high school, so he became a teenage mascot, a bat boy that sang "Take Me Out to the Ballgame" and got used to pleasing crowds of people.

But when the game was over and the postgame show finally wrapped up, there was yelling and physical abuse waiting for him in the parking lot.

He graduated high school with scars—real ones and invisible emotional ones. The real ones healed and made him look tough with his shirt off. The invisible ones never did and made him crazy and unstable and desperate when he was on a binge.

Billy met a lot of people on the fringe of the entertainment industry that did promotions at the minor league stadium. He found his way into comedy and landed a spot with the Ouch! Potatoes. In season one, with the group riding high and getting good reviews, Billy kept his demons in check. In season two, after a couple of rough shows, he got out of control one night and basically blacked out on stage, though they were able to pass it off as part of the act. He got a warning and a suggestion to consider professional help. After that he held it together for a couple of shows, but the demons got the best of him and he ended up punching a heckler in the face.

The Potatoes were down to eight and a half members and limped through the rest of the second season. During that last month, Gene observed Dave come into his own while the rest of the show and the group itself were, on good nights, mediocre, with fans leaving like gamblers walking away from a table after suffering a modest loss. They didn't win, but in a way they'd been entertained and the time had passed more or less pleasantly.

*

But to Gene, Dave was hilarious. Gene was always able to keep a straight face on stage, but Dave pushed him to the edge of breaking. He was on fire. He was making jokes that people weren't always catching, the humor on a slightly different wavelength, but sometimes, on certain nights, a portion of the audience would get dialed in and Dave would have them in tears. For this slice of people, he was killing it, while at the same time he was perfecting his timing, tweaking his techniques, and slowly expanding the wedge of audience that was really getting him. It was like a fighter gaining confidence, and only the people that truly knew and studied fighting could see the potential. And while he was developing, occasionally, he delivered a big uppercut that no one saw coming.

Gene's role, in contrast, was that of a facilitator. He was like the point guard on a basketball team—keeping everyone involved. Occasionally, it fell to the point guard to make the play, and in these moments, Gene delivered caustic and witty lines. But only occasionally. He was like a limited player that relied on others to create his shot. More often, he was setting someone else up. Which is how he liked it. Lobbing one over to Dave to slam home.

No one really said it, but it was on the strength of these alley-oops that the Ouch! Potatoes earned a third season from the Last Laugh. It was a big deal because it meant eking out survival in show business:

two shows a week in LA plus a third on the road. They were traveling up and down the coast in a van, going as far north as Vancouver and as far south as Tijuana. They got paid.

But season three was different. Instead of being the main draw, they were now opening for other acts and comedy troupes. They were playing clubs and theaters that weren't as nice and didn't sell out. They were occasionally sent off the beaten track to small cities that weren't photogenic enough for a postcard.

The third season was brutal. The Last Laugh took control of the Ouch! Potatoes and subbed in five new comedians. Instead of chemistry, there was animosity. Everyone was competing for laughs, and there was a clear dividing line between the old and the new Potatoes. It was a tug-of-war. A fight over pie. An ego battle over phantom fame. It was tense, awkward, and ugly everywhere—in the van, rehearsing, and onstage.

There was no common ground, no rapport, no feel, and no depth to any of the material. It was the most dreaded word in comedy—forced. And the only ones who felt it more keenly than the audience were the performers. Gene felt it severely. He was now the point guard on a team of ball hogs. Whomever he passed it to, they shot it, open or not. There was no team game so Gene disappeared. He didn't have the personality or the charisma to score one-on-one with an audience—so he went entire shows without scoring any laughs.

Dave tried to carry the show, and some nights came close. But it was impossible. The new Potatoes broke the cardinal rule of improv: "yes and." This rule states that you cannot say no. If your partner starts a scene off with "Isn't this ice cream parlor the best? I love gluten-free, sugarless, dairy-free, iceless, creamless ice cream!" then you must start your line with "Yes and …" You cannot say no. You cannot deny the parlor or the ice cream or anything your partner scoops onto the stage.

But in season three, the new Potatoes said no all the time. They said no to lines, ideas, scenes, plots, and character developments. They said no to imaginary props, open-armed invitations, unicycle rides, vegan jazz, and blowing out candles on birthday cakes. The last straw was when one of the new Potatoes said no to a prosthetic limb.

The reviews were brutal and spot-on. The audience said no with their entertainment dollars. And halfway through the third season, the Last Laugh said no and the Ouch! Potatoes were cooked.

They offered Dave a spot in another troupe and Gene a spot teaching Improv 1, level A. Dave and Gene were having dinner one night on the pier when they both decided it was time to say "No and" to improv.

NO. 5
BEER GIRL

Jimmy and Mike sat waiting in the fairway of the par 5 11th at Twin Oaks.

"It was dumb luck," Jimmy said. "I had four interviews for my residency. Three in Chicago and one at UCSD. The UCSD one was right after Gene's wedding. I gave a best man speech, got shit-faced, took a day to sleep it off, went surfing, and then interviewed at UCSD."

"What's your PhD in?" Mike asked.

"Neuropsychology," Jimmy said. "So you rank your favorites, and they rank you, and then you get placed. I ranked UCSD fourth. But still, that's how the dice landed."

"Interesting," Mike said.

"It doesn't feel that long ago," Jimmy said. "But now we're out here in San Diego, with jobs and families and mortgages. Man, life is an ass-kicker. We're lucky we have friends and get to go outside and play."

"How's the golf/surf deal with Gene working out?"

"Good. I take him surfing one week, he takes me golfing the next. He's not catching any waves. I'm not getting any pars. It's a pretty even exchange. It's good to have new hobbies that you suck at. Keeps you grounded. By the way, thanks for taking me out today. My goal is to beat Nick, because I know how much losing pisses him off."

The group ahead cleared. Jimmy jumped out of the cart. "What should I hit?"

"You're 200 out, maybe keep that seven iron going?"

Jimmy pulled out his seven iron and, with an uneven tempo, hit a slicing wormburner that rolled 40 yards downhill into the right rough. He wasn't fazed in the least.

"How about you?" Jimmy asked, plopping back down into the cart. "When did you start playing golf?"

"Only a few years ago," Mike said, driving up to his ball in the left rough. "I started meeting with these cruise ship bigwigs, for my business. All we would do is golf. I found that the better I played, the more musicians they put on their ships. So I got the bug."

"Interesting," Jimmy said. He took a hit from his vaporizer. "You get a birdie, that's a trombone player."

"Pretty much."

Mike addressed his ball, 175 yards out. But he had an angle through the trees. He hit his approach to the left fringe. As he put his six iron back in his bag haphazardly, he smacked his ring finger in between two irons. It immediately began to swell painfully around his wedding ring.

He wasn't that worried about his score when he three-putted from ten feet.

"I think I broke my finger," he said aloud.

Jimmy picked up after skulling one out of the trap and went into the bushes to pee. At the 12th tee, the beer girl pulled up and Mike bought two tallboys.

"Ah," he said, gripping the beers. "The cold feels good."

"What happened?" the beer girl asked.

"Oh, just jammed my finger between clubs."

"Let me take a look at it," she said. "That looks bad." She was probably in her midfifties.

She grabbed a plastic cup, scooped it full of ice, and gave it to Mike. He pinned the cup between the two beers like a waiter. Jimmy walked up.

"You keep your finger in this ice," she said. "And don't drink it when it melts. It's dirty from sitting in the well of my cart."

Jimmy, sensing something awry, looked at Mike holding the two beers and the cup of ice. He honed in on the red, swollen finger around the cup of ice with flecks of dirt in it.

The beer girl drove off with a wave.

"Did she just tell you not to drink her dirty cart ice water?"

"Yep," Mike said. "Indeed she did."

"Thanks, Mom," Jimmy joked, pretending to call after her. "I was gonna drink your dirty cart ice water until you said that. Good looking out. Do you know if they use chemicals to treat the fairways here, in case I want to lick a divot later?"

Mike put the beers in the cup holders and his red, swollen finger in the ice. It felt good.

NO. 6
PEEING IN THE BUSHES

Metropolis Writers Workshop
Online Stand-Up Comedy Course Level B
Assignment #2
Gene Santos

June 21st, 2017

All right, good evening everybody. It's a pleasure to be here. I would like to get things going with a little audience participation, to get you guys engaged and contributing before you're too drunk and just start laughing at my back sweat.

No, just kidding. I'm not much of a sweater. I have some friends, though—boy, look out when they get under the lights. They don't make deodorant that strong. Wearing a suit to a wedding during the summer? Forget about it. But don't worry. They're doing tests on rhinoceroses I think, so maybe my buddy will be able to wear that blue button-down at his sister's wedding next month after all. Keep your fingers crossed.

(To a straight-faced member of the audience.) Oh, what, you don't think they should be testing deodorant on rhinos? No, that's fair. We all have our principles. If only there wasn't so much money to be made in preventing back sweat and swass. That's a scientific term, there, if you're not familiar. Swass is the sweat that comes from your ass. A little nugget of education for ya.

All right, so here we go. I say a topic, and then I tailor my set in terms of time, subject matter, and the relative brow of the humor, based on the audience response. That's right. You, the audience, are in control here. It's like those books—Choose Your Own Adventure. But instead of time travel or dragons, we're doing something far more out-there: Choose Your Own Comedy.

Let's give it a shot. I say the topic, and you respond based on your interest. It's an experiment. Like if you really like it, you would cheer or go bananas, and if you think it's going to suck you would stay quiet or boo. Yes, I'm really inviting you to heckle me.

Without further ado, here goes: My first topic will be (drum roll please) … BONERS.

Possible responses:

1.   If audience goes wild
2.   If audience is divided
3.   If audience is hostile, rude, or apathetic

1) Middle and high school kids are in trouble. I mean books are going away in schools. It's all tablets and smart boards and smart desks and other smart things that will probably just make the teachers feel dumb. It's a real nationwide epidemic—middle and high school kids will have nothing to hide their boners with. I mean, gosh, did we have it good. In my day we had three-ring six-inch binders to hide our quarter-inch boners. Those binders were mammoth. You could hide a python behind those things. Seriously. We were lucky. Sure, there was no internet and we had to use a card catalog, type on typewriters, and learn stuff like the Dewey Decimal system and cursive. But at least we could hide our boners when we walked down the hall. Kids today have it rough.

I find it hard to believe that the writers of that show *Growing Pains* really wanted to name Kirk Cameron's, a.k.a. Mike's, friend Boner. I mean these are talented, serious TV sitcom writers that make good money, and that's what they come up with for the nickname of his friend? Boner? Really? I think what happened is that one of the writers got fired. They let him go right before the pilot got accepted and he got the royal screw. Like he did a lot of the writing and contributed some solid ideas at the old writer's table, and then right before the show started making cash, they realized they had one too many writers on the payroll and this guy was for some reason expendable. I bet the dude, in a haze of vindictive anger, broke into the writer's room, grabbed the script just before it was going to final press, and changed the friend's nickname from Buddy or Dude to Boner. Then the next day at reading it was too late to change it and they filmed it and they were stuck. I mean seriously. How else do they name an adolescent boy's best friend Boner? Sure, you know the ardent fan that sits around his basement eating frozen waffles all day can tell me that the kid's last name was Stabone, but I don't buy it. Somewhere, some fired TV writer is laughing his ass off.

2) OK, I can see a division in the audience. Now I know that we've got both the high and the low brow. People are drinking either top shelf liquor or Miller High Life. Don't let the name fool you. Any time "high" is used in beer, it means low. It's mathematical. Anyway, don't worry, I know where my base is. I'm like Trump. You low brows, go ahead and get comfortable. Order another High Life.

But first let me address the high brows: What, boner humor isn't good enough for you elitists? Perched up there on your top shelf, looking down on boner jokes? "I shan't laugh at this erectile humor! I simply shan't!" You guys are probably the same people that don't laugh at farts. Like someone lets out a real squeaker—one of those high-pitchers that sounds like a horn—and you can't even smile? Or you're offended by the sound. It bothers your delicate sensibilities. If a chair amplifies some deep butt thunder and makes it really loud, you're stone-faced, just absolutely without mirth. Or if it's a real stinker that you can tell has a hint of gorgonzola cheese—like you can taste the gorgonzola—you can't even find the humor to give yourself a little relief from the raunchy stench. That's what America has become.

Wait a minute, I think I just stumbled on what's dividing America. Farts and boners. Eureka! If I can get one half of the country laughing at farts and boners, and the other half maybe toning it down a little, JUST a little, like holding it in once in a while, or at least farting near open windows, maybe we can get this healthcare thing figured out. I'll run for office and that'll be my platform: Make Farts Funny Again!

(In Jim Gaffigan audience-voice imitation style) I thought he was going to talk about boners, but now he's talking about farts. It's like every joke leads to farts with this guy. What kind of topic is that to build an act around?

3) Sorry, sorry, I didn't realize so many people here had ED. (Whisper: erectile dysfunction.) Go ahead. Keep smiling on the outside, but we know you're crying on the inside. It's a real affliction! I should've known with all the Viagra wrappers in the men's room garbage. Aren't those commercials the worst? They're on like every ten minutes of every football game. Thanks for ruining football Sunday. It was bad enough not having sex, but now football is gone too. Oh, I'll just watch golf—nope, that's ruined too. The advertising execs are just rubbing our noses in it. Basically any men's programming. Is there any man out there who doesn't know Viagra exists? That would be like not knowing electricity exists. Oh, like some Rip Van Winkle is going to be watching Sunday Night Football and see a commercial and be like, "IT'S A MIRACLE!"

I have empathy for you guys and, what the hell, the wives too. It must suck when that starts to go. Losing hair, gaining weight, kidney failure? No biggie. Can't get hard? Wow, getting older sucks! And those commercials. I mean besides being cheesy—like the middle-aged but still attractive couple making eyes as the guy opens a bottle of wine? Seriously, could they get someone from the porn industry on that marketing team? Is that too much to ask?

It's terrifying too. Chest pain? Erections lasting more than 24 hours? What's in those things? Gorilla glue? Geez. And why is it 24 hours that's the problem? I mean, if you're going on hour three of an erection, isn't that time to raise the red flag? I mean, you go through breakfast, get to work, have a productive morning, you're in the break room grabbing a cup of coffee, the whole time pitching a tent … that doesn't raise any kind of alarm?

INSTRUCTOR FEEDBACK:

Great work here, Gene! I love the audience participation format—a fantastic technique to simultaneously gauge the audience and get them invested in your routine. You've chosen some very reliable and established material in farts, boners, and Viagra. The challenge is to present the comedy with a fresh and unique angle. The loss of books and binders does exactly that. Nice job!

I'm not so sure you accomplished this freshness with the Viagra and farts topics. Dividing the audience is a risky move. It can pay off, if the divided segment that you target your jokes at is small and the humor is accurate, true, and deserved. But if the supportive portion of your audience is anything close to even 33%, then you risk alienating a significant portion of the people that you're trying to make laugh. Dangerous territory indeed.

There's a lot of funny material here, though—the *Growing Pains* reference, comparing farts and boners to what's actually dividing America, and the ubiquity of Viagra commercials. The key for your rewrite will be how to tweak your format so that a paucity of audience members will find themselves in the crosshairs.

Also, final note: I believe it's "*Creature* from the Black Lagoon." A classic!

-Rob

NO. 7
SNACK BAR

Metropolis Writers Workshop
Online Stand-Up Comedy Course Level B
Assignment #3
Gene Santos

June 28th, 2017

This afternoon I was sitting there, eating a sandwich, when I read the back of the mustard bottle.

(Pause for audience reaction.)

What? Are you against literacy? Are you one of those non-readers? Stop reading food labels, next thing you know you're attending a book-burning rally.

So yeah. I'm a *voracious* reader. I always have something with me to read. I'm a third of the way through a Cocoa Puffs box right now. It's pretty dense, but fascinating.

Anyway, it says on the back of the mustard bottle how they use 100% natural ingredients. Like that's something to brag about.

"Try our mustard! It's better than the competitor that mixes in lead and plastic!" 100% natural. Like there's some math guy that adds it up. He's at the end of the assembly line. "It's 100%, I counted."

Or if they were at 99%, would they really tell you? "That other 1%, don't worry about it. Now where did I throw that used condom?"

Then the label said, "A secret blend of spices and vinegar, for the perfect balance of flavor and tang."

Secret? It's mustard. How secret can it be?

Like there's a Russian special ops out there trying to crack a real American secret: the recipe for mustard! But they just can't figure it out. It's something they've kept SECRET since 1869.

And what are those spices? Don't tell the Russians, but it's salt and pepper.

Secret blend. I bet the guy writing the label was rereading it and was like, "It's good, but it's missing something. Hmmm, oh I've got it … What if the blend of spices is somehow mysterious, like A SECRET?"

The only guy he told is the mathematician at the end of the line. "Hey, don't tell the rest of marketing, but I changed 'blend of spices' to 'secret blend of spices.'"

The math guy was probably like, "I don't know, I'm terrible at keeping secrets. Especially when the word 'secret' is in the secret."

Good thing no one ever reads the label on the mustard bottle. Until today!

INSTRUCTOR FEEDBACK:

Gene, this is a great example of everyday, observational humor. Nice job! You've done excellent work pointing out the ridiculous and absurd. This piece has some real potential to develop pivots or work in some comedic circles, topics from our reading assignments this week.

As far as the used condom joke goes, for me personally, it was a little too much surprise. Remember the quote from this week's online lecture: "Comedy is confounding expectations in a way that makes sense." Sometimes you can knock your audience so far off guard that you lose them. The only way to find out with some jokes is by trial and error.

Also, as we discussed in our online lecture, this humor needs to be developed, aged—like a fine mustard! Sometimes our humor needs a little push, an oomph, to get from kind of funny to where we want it: funny as hell. I'm sure you're up for the task and I look forward to seeing this piece revised.

Keep up the good work!

-Rob

AN EXTRA CHIP
IN THE BAG

Metropolis Writers Workshop
Online Stand-Up Comedy Course Level B
Assignment #4
Gene Santos

July 5th, 2017

As a guy, you can't really call out your friends when they hurt your feelings. It's not a guy thing. We let each other down and sweep it under the rug.

I mean sure, things are changing and gender roles are becoming more fluid and all that. But if you call a guy out for hurting your feelings, it's still a "chick move." Turn in your man card and confess that your balls are tiny pebbles.

"Hey dude, can you grab me a beer while you're up? Oh, and why didn't you come to my birthday party last week?"

"What?"

"Yeah, you said you were going to come but then you didn't."

"Oh, uh, yeah, um. Sorry man, my kid got sick and my wife had to work."

"Bullshit! I've been to your Birthday Palooza for six years running and you can't stop by for one drink? Where's this relationship heading? I don't even know where this friendship is anymore."

"Dude, did you just grow a uterus?"

"My bad. My bad. It's cool that you didn't come to my birthday party and that you don't respond to my texts and that you always change plans so that they're in your best interest. So you going to grab that beer or what?"

Another thing guys can't do with their guy friends is bring up old shit. It's a very non-macho, low testosterone move. Doesn't wear well at a bachelor party or a guys' night.

"OK Steve, you're single blind, and Bill, you're the double. And speaking of double blinds, Bill, why didn't you come to my wedding?"

"Your wedding? That was eight years ago. What are you talking about?"

"Well, you could've at least sent a toaster oven. Pot's good?"

So when my friends bail out at the last minute or do something unfriend-like, my wife is always trying to get me to call them out. She thinks I'm being soft or letting them run over me, like it has something to do with my spine. But I think it's just a guy thing. We don't really sweat that stuff. And I think it's because it's impossible to do so without sounding like a 15-year-old girl.

"I thought we were supposed to watch 12 hours of football together."

"It really bothers me that we haven't eaten encased meats together recently!"

"I find it disconcerting that we don't binge drink ourselves into oblivion with regularity!"

Just try and say something like that without sounding like a high school girl. I dare you.

INSTRUCTOR FEEDBACK:

Gene, I love the subject matter! "Chick moves" could be an entire setlist. You've done a nice job using your authentic self by bringing in how your wife tells you to confront your friends. Also, there is nice comedic conflict between trying to be a "macho guy" but also talking about your hurt feelings. This is very RELATABLE. There are also nice elements of surprise, exaggeration, and absurdity.

As you rewrite this premise, consider honing your click-points, a topic we discussed in this week's lecture. How can you improve the overall flow? How can the examples be tightened, sharpened? Also, just a thought, in order to maximize the laughter, could you show the other side of the coin, i.e., how your wife deals with a friend letting her down? This would be tricky, but perhaps could be a nice pivot.

-Rob

NO. 8
A DRY BALL WASHER

Subject line: Checking In

1 message

Rob Wiley <rwiley@metrowriters.com>
Tue, Nov 7, 2017 at 8:28 PM
To: Genesantos17@gmail.com

Hi Gene,

I wanted to reach out because you have yet to chime in on the message board for level C and I haven't received the first two assignments. I'm hoping you've been busy at open mics!

If you're having doubts about continuing with our stand-up writing courses, I figured, in addition to your current classmates, I should jump in as one more voice encouraging you to keep at it.

I for one am eager to see you develop some of the ideas from the final assignment of level B: 100 Nuggets. Particularly, the Hyperbole Ha #19, the older generation's exaggerated excitement and fulfillment from using the carpool lane to beat traffic and arrive early for a flight! Makes me think of my father-in-law☺ Or Juxtaposition Joke #56, two families from the Be Kind movement at lunch in Disneyland with only one table available. So good!

In fact, after looking over your ideas I felt compelled to reread some of your old assignments, all the way back to level A's finding outrage that is bite-size and palatable, i.e. a Coors lite can on the side of the road that someone should have recycled. Funny! It really stuck out to me, your improvement from level A to level B, and I think you could make similar strides in level C, not to mention the benefit of added rep's with our new video segments.

Finally, on a personal note, as a middle-aged working stiff and a father, I think you should continue for one last very important reason: people in our stage of life really need comic relief! From your experiences as a teacher, parent, and easy-going 40-something, I believe you have something unique to offer people eager for laughter. To take it one step further (an ode to our class code of going the honest AND vulnerable distance), there's some nights when I'm tired, beyond sleep-deprived, and reading amateur stand-up is about the last thing I'm in the mood for. But your work always brightened my day. And I'm not just writing that because they pay me to keep the customers happy;)

If you can't join our current level, please consider signing up for level C at a future date and (in Yoda voice) *complete your training you must.* Please be aware that refunds must be requested before the completion of week 4.

Your stand-up compadre,
Rob Wiley

NO. 9
THE LINKS LIGHTER
PART TWO:
FINISH IN DARKNESS

Thursday, November 2nd, 2017

Nick Moy sat on his couch in the dark playing a video game. A wet washcloth with the Chinese symbol for good fortune, pronounced fú, lay across his forehead. He was playing an old version of *Madden NFL* so he could use the 1985 Bears. His opponent was the 1976 Steelers. The game was scoreless in the fourth quarter. He ran a sweep with Walter Payton and did a spin move around Mean Joe Green, but Jack Ham caught him at the line of scrimmage. His phone buzzed. He paused the game facing a third and long.

"Hey babe," he said.

"How are you feeling?" his wife, Ashley, asked.

"Better. The headache is almost gone."

"That's good. Did you sleep?"

"No," Nick said. "I took my meds and rested."

"You need to see your neurologist again. They're becoming more frequent."

"I think it's stress-related. Us buying a house. The job interview. Just a lot going on."

"I thought they were going to call you today," Ashley said.

"They said this week. If not today, maybe tomorrow."

"Did you take your other meds? You know, to help your boys swim?"

"Oh, right," Nick said. "I forgot. I'll take one now."

"I have to get back to class. Remember, I'm going over to Julie's tonight to watch *The Bachelor* so you're on your own for dinner. Unless you want me to cancel."

"No," Nick said. "You should go. I'm feeling better. I'll just watch the Thursday night game."

"I figured as much. You rest. I love you."

"Love you."

Nick went into the bathroom and found what they referred to as his "sperm pills." He picked up a capsule and remembered the doctor saying they were "to improve both morphology and motility, the structure and motion."

"Time to morph up down there," he said to his reflection.

Nick swallowed the pill and went back to his spot on the couch. He weighed his options to get out of the third and long situation—a draw versus a play action pass. He selected a weak flood passing play and paused the game to check his email. He closed his eyes and focused on taking a deep breath, trying to dissociate himself from the intensity of his headache. He opened his eyes, and the top message caught his attention. He opened it and read:

"Nick, this is Alister Huff from the Ed Bavera Fire Investigation Company. Congratulations. We would like to offer you the position of arson investigator. If you accept, please stop in tomorrow and we'll go over the paperwork."

Nick closed his email and texted Ashley that he got the job, then unpaused the game.

Jim McMahon dropped back to pass. In an instant, three Steelers converged on him. He tried to throw at the last moment, but it was too late. The Steelers forced a fumble and returned it for a touchdown. Nick grimaced as what felt like an ice pick jabbed his brain.

Sunday, November 5th, 2017

Gene put his old smartphone in the desk drawer. He unplugged the glue gun and propped it up against the base of the lamp on the desk, with the hot metal tip suspended. He switched the lamp on and walked back to his golf bag near the bed. Now all the lights were on in the hotel room with the shades drawn tight. It was the middle of the afternoon.

Phineas poured hot water from the coffee maker into his mug. "Incredible," he said. He ran his finger along the cord from the coffee maker to the outlet. "Just incredible." He unplugged and plugged and unplugged again, examining the metal of the male part. His lips repeated the syllables of his new word. "E-lek-tri-si-tee. Remember, Rod, repetition is an aid to memory." He gave the empty socket a final rub with his thumb, inserted the plug, and moved on to dropping a bag of tea in the steaming water. "And tea in little bags." He picked up the mug with one hand and his tamping iron with the other. He walked past Gene digging through his golf bag, then glanced curiously at the glue gun. He went around the bed and set the mug down on the nightstand.

"Here's a task right here, Rod," he said, indicating the unmade bed. He put the tamping iron on the bed and removed his overcoat, folding it up and draping it over the back of an upholstered arm chair he had pulled out from the corner. He ran his hand over the fabric, comparing it to the other chair near the desk. He compiled the sensory data with his growing fascination over modern materials. Before sitting down, he adjusted his bow tie in the mirror. Once seated, he reached over and picked up the iron. "Simple tasks will help him forge those lost connections."

Gene muttered a curse word as he rooted through the pockets of his golf bag.

"The irritability is back," Phineas said, laying the iron across his lap. "Now, now, take it easy." He held up the iron in his arms, cradling it. "I don't like sleeping on the floor any more than you do, Rod. Yes. It would be nice to have a bed to sleep in at night. It would've been *thoughtful*. But let's remember, we've only been with Gene two days. Two days since his accident. That was about the time we began our descent, if memory serves, down into that little pit of delirium. Days of madness, howls, gnashing teeth … How many days until we became rational again? Five? Six? It all blurs together."

Gene returned to the desk and set down a bag of tees and a jar containing small red spheres.

"If you recall, Rod, we also underestimated our damage," Phineas said. "Remember when the first doctor arrived at the tavern? My famous line: 'Here's business enough for you.' He didn't believe me, whatever his name was. Doc William Something. Not until I vomited."

Phineas held up his mug to the light and watched the steam. "Once he saw half a teacup of brain spurt through the exit hole on top of my head, he changed his tune pretty quick. Hard to argue with spattered globs of gray matter." He held the mug to his lips, blew on it, and took a small sip. "It must have made a horrid sound hitting the floor."

Gene went back to his golf bag. Phineas resumed blowing on the surface of the hot liquid.

"It's the pressure. Not good. All these symptoms we are observing. The rudeness, that's not Gene. The headaches. Impatience. All of them. Just look at the swelling on his forehead. Still red. His mind must be under enormous pressure."

Gene came back to the desk and set down a mortar, a pestle, and a small white container.

"I don't blame him for being frustrated with us," Phineas said, taking another sip.

Gene stood, lost in thought.

"When Doc Harlow arrived an hour later, he didn't believe it either. Not until his fingers touched inside my head," Phineas said with a chortle. He rubbed the top of his skull. "Later that night I told Harlow I expected to be at work in a few days." He laughed. "A few days—can you imagine?" Then he spoke up, toward Gene. "There's another similarity: denial. We both denied the severity."

Gene went back over to the golf bag and resumed rooting through the pockets.

"I know you don't like all the gory talk, Rod. The vomiting, the loose and open bandages, all the drainage. Doc Harlow saved my life. Proof that Gene needs to be under a doctor's care." He extended the tamping iron to the window and lifted the curtain, looking out at the hotel parking lot fenced with palm trees blowing in the breeze. Spots of bright sunlight dazzled off the mirrors and surfaces of the cars, causing Phineas to squint. "Amazing. These automobiles."

"Dammit, Phin—I said to keep the shades drawn!" Gene shouted over his shoulder.

Phineas pulled the tamping iron back. "Please, I prefer Phineas," he said. "That other fellow, he's more of a Phin. He doesn't act like a proper gentleman, or dress like one for that matter. Reprehensible behavior, to be sure. He can't control himself. My advice: Ignore his antics."

Gene turned back to his golf bag and opened a different pocket. "Here they are," he said, pulling out two black film canisters. He walked back to the desk, took another cell phone from his pocket, and sat down in the desk chair. He arranged the canisters and phone on the desk along with the bag of tees, the white container, the mortar and pestle, and the jar full of red spheres, taking care not to touch the tip of the hot glue gun.

Phineas spoke in a low voice to his iron. "I bore it all with 'heroic firmness,' according to Harlow. So far, Rod, we've seen Gene's firmness. But heroic? That remains to be seen. If we don't do anything about the pressure, I fear for our new friend. Remember, according to Doc Harlow, on the second day I was 'decidedly delirious.' Then back to rational on the fourth." He picked up and examined the alarm clock. "Day twelve was when the infection set in, though the man had little concept of what an infection is. Semi-comatose. I walked right up to the edge of darkness. The coffin was ready. But Harlow saved me again. Treated the infection. Drained eight ounces of pus. 'Horribly fetid' were his words, I believe." He put down the clock. "Oh, don't be such a baby," he said, slapping the iron.

"Unlike Gene here, I wanted to be around my family," Phineas said. "And I enjoyed seeing my friends. Remember, once I got over the infection, Harlow said I was 'uncontrollable' by my friends because I wanted to go home and get back to my family. I was only twenty-five! Going out in all kinds of weather, no overcoat, thin boots, looking for my mother and my uncle." He flicked the switch of the lamp near him—off, on, off, on. "Right now, we're the only friends Gene's got. We'll stay and help him. Once we release the pressure, I'm sure he'll have the same desire."

*

"Dammit," Nick said from his couch in the dark. His headache throbbed. He was nauseous but forced down a sip of water for his dry mouth. The performance of his fantasy football team, the Suey Choppers, wasn't helping. He had picked up the Buffalo Bills defense and special teams from the waiver wire. A group that, despite the favorable matchup, had just allowed a Matt Forte ten-yard touchdown and now trailed 24–7. His phone buzzed with a text. It was his opponent for this week, Harris, who also happened to have Forte.

HS: another tuddy. double dippin

NM: shut it

HS: Missed you at Rosie's last Monday. Good times. The boys were in rare form.

NM: Was at the interview

HS: Did you get the job?

NM: Yep. New title: Nick Moy, Arson Investigator. On the job training starts next week.

HS: Congrats.

Nick looked down at the dots, waiting to see if Harris had anything else to say.

HS: Can you believe that Zach Miller play on Sunday? Should have been a tuddy. Never mind that he tore an artery in his leg and almost had to have it amputated. Ref says he has to survive the ground. That he lost control of the ball and it was the right call. Complete shit. Survive the ground? He almost didn't survive period.

"Oh, come on," Nick shouted to his empty apartment. The Bills, now on offense, fumbled. He picked up his fú washcloth and rubbed his temple.

HS: Tough injury in a tough season. Nice choice BTW with the Bills D

NM: Bears are done.

HS: No surrender! Who is hosting Bear Down for next week?

NM: Bears on bye.

HS: Oh forgot. Want to carpool to Rosie's for MNF?

NM: Going to take a bye myself this week from football. Gotta focus on the new job and the move to new house.

HS: OK. Go get 'em.

"Shit!" Nick cried as Forte dove in for another tuddy. He reached for another almotriptin, his migraine medication, and turned away from the TV. The light was hurting his eyes.

*

Gene picked up the glue gun as the iconic riff ignited the first song on his playlist, Jimi Hendrix's "Fire." He spread hot glue over the sides of the extra long, extra wide wooden tee. Then he reached into a jar full of match heads: small bright red spheres with white eyes, like something you might use on decoys.

"No. Stop right there," Gene said. "We are *not* the same."

He scooped a handful of the match heads and spread them out. He resealed the jar and painstakingly set about placing a row of them along each side of the tee. He began at the pointy tip, working along the thin tan shaft, which was half a centimeter in diameter, so that each match head just fit. When he reached the bowl-shaped head of the tee, he rotated the shaft and started again. It was slow work. "Fire" ended.

"… both of us thrust into an odd kind of fame," Phineas was saying from his chair in the corner, swirling the last sip of tea in his mug. "We both suffered trauma to our left frontal lobe. Irrevocable trauma. At least, that's what Doc Harlow said."

"Sleep Now in the Fire" by Rage Against the Machine began and Gene turned up the volume, drowning Phineas out. Gene finished the last row of match heads as the song ended. The match heads made four continuous white lines along the tee's shaft—roughly a dozen heads to each line. He took a moment to enjoy the symmetry.

"… forever bonded by the cruel and wanton hand of Fate," Gene heard Phineas say.

"No," Gene said, looking up at him in the mirror. He paused the Talking Heads tune "Burning Down the House." "That rod in your hands went through your skull. You can't open one of your eyes. There's a scar on your face. Spread your hair apart and it reveals a pulsating brain. I got hit by a golf ball. We're not the same, Phin."

"Please. Phineas. And sure, ol' Rod here went through my head," he said, holding up the tamping iron. "Even if the exit point is disagreed upon by scholars. In fact, some ignoramuses have called you a crowbar, Rod. Isn't that ridiculous? A crowbar with a *curved* end. But no matter. Gene. Our brains. Our minds. Therein the similarity lies."

Gene turned the music back on. He rubbed his temple, turned down the volume, and filled the surface on top of the tee. Five match heads fit snugly on the small concave area normally occupied by a golf ball, creating a pentagon of circles. He took another moment to enjoy his handiwork—both the tactile and the visual.

"Well, what do you think?" he said, tossing it over.

"Interesting," Phineas said. "Different from my day." He leaned the tamping iron against the wall and regarded the match heads. "Of course, you're not exactly blowing up rock for a railroad track. But I guess for your purposes—which I strongly urge you to reconsider—it could do the trick."

Gene reached over to pick up the mortar and pestle and then set about grinding match heads. He finished those and then did a second handful to AC/DC's "Shot Down in Flames." He created a mixture by carefully pouring the ground match heads along with a powder from the white container into the two large black plastic film canisters.

Phineas came over and eyed the powder. "What is it?" he asked.

"It's pyrotechnic powder. It's used in fireworks."

"Py-ro-tek-nik. Interesting," Phineas said. "So very interesting. Progress in almost every facet of life. Just amazing."

"Yeah, well, life goes on. Or something," Gene said as "Shot Down in Flames" ended.

"Can we watch more television?" Phineas said, feeling the large screen with his fingertips.

When no answer came, Phineas put the tee back on the desk. "I just thought of another similarity," he said, stepping back by the bed. He picked up the iron and twirled it.

Gene took the tee and sprinkled powder from the canisters on the match heads, which stuck to the still-tacky glue. The Clash's "London's Burning" started.

"Both cases involve a cart," Phineas said. "You were carried in a golf cart. I rode in an oxcart. Of course, my ride was over a kilometer." He tapped Gene playfully with the tamping iron. He waited for a response. When none came, he frowned and adjusted his bow tie.

Gene rose and put the tee inside a case for sunglasses, then put the case and the canisters with the mix of crushed up match heads and pyrotechnic powder neatly into his golf bag pocket. Phineas followed him. He set down the tamping iron and pulled out the driver.

"What did you say this metal was?"

"Titanium," Gene replied. He was searching through the other pockets of his golf bag. "Where did I put—?" The music ended.

Phineas tapped the head of the driver on the tamping iron. "What do you think of this, Rod? Pretty impressive craftsmanship. All in the name of recreation. Golf, it's called." He slid the driver back into the golf bag. He flicked the face of the driver, then moved to the irons. "What did you call these? Irons?" He waited but there was no answer. Gene continued searching. "But they're not made of real iron. I suppose iron would be too heavy. Besides, he says this metal, this titanium, is the best for sparks. And as we know, Rod, that's all it takes. One spark."

Gene was digging through his golf bag. Tees, balls, markers, and ball repair tools jangled inside the pockets.

Phineas picked up the wastebasket and examined pieces of shredded credit cards. "Amazing, isn't it, Rod?"

"Don't you ever shut up?" Gene said, moving across the room and opening his suitcase.

"I wasn't talking to you," Phineas replied over his shoulder. "Sudden mood swings, another characteristic," he said to the tamping iron with his head tilted and an eyebrow raised. He held up a shred of credit card with a magnetic strip to the light, examined it, and tossed it back in the garbage. "Imagine, Rod, a little card that can be used for money. A credit card, he calls it, made of, what was it? Plas-tik? Where do these materials come from? Simply amazing." He set the basket down and walked back to the upholstered arm chair in the corner. Gene was on his knees looking under the bed. He pulled out a large canvas bag, unzipped it, rifled through its contents, and zipped it back up. Then he went into the bathroom.

Phineas sidled over to the bag. He used the tamping iron to slide open the zipper.

He whistled. "That's a lot of cash," he said. Gene rushed back into the room, grabbed the bag, and zipped it back up.

"Stay out of my things," he said. Phineas jumped back and stood by the window.

"And get away from the window!"

"Irritable, aggressive," Phineas said, moving back to the mirror. "Check two more boxes, Rod." Then, to the tamping iron's reflection, "Irrational thinking, too, if this bag is any indication. It looks like the bag of someone on a path from which there's no turning back. It's the pressure. If we can release it, we can return him to his right mind."

Gene dropped to his knees and searched under the desk. Phineas sat down on the bed but then quickly popped back up.

"Holes!" Phineas exclaimed. "Both our calamities involved holes. Mine surged forth from a hole and yours surged toward a hole."

"You're reaching now," Gene said. He stood up and held his head in his hands. "Where in the hell did I put it?"

"Memory loss. Another similarity, Rod."

Phineas stepped toward Gene with two hands on his tamping iron. He set it across Gene's chest, lightly pressing it and turning him so that they stood face-to-face. Gene alternated his stare between Phineas's good and bad eye.

"What I was saying earlier," Phineas said, "in the parking lot while we were waiting for the Mexican man who sold you that automobile—I meant it. Every word. I did it and so can you. You can find a way to live. You can recover. Your whole life and personality are not restricted to one area of your frontal lobe. See a doctor. Get back to your family. With the right structure and care, you can relearn all that you've lost. You can even teach again. There is hope."

Gene pushed away the tamping iron.

"Look at what I was able to do," Phineas said, smacking his hand with the rod for emphasis. "A hundred and fifty years ago. Don't believe the myths. I worked plenty. I made a recovery. Nearly twelve more years of life. Think of—"

"We're not the same, Gage!" Gene screamed. He squeezed both hands into fists, then froze. "Oh. Right." He walked over to the desk and pulled open a drawer. He pulled out his worn and cracked smartphone. Then he set it on the desk, took the pestle, and smashed it. He forcefully ground the pieces down then used his arm to brush the fragments into the wastebasket.

He went over to his new phone, sat on the bed, and started a new song. First, though, he had to listen to an ad since he hadn't created an account on the streaming service. Then he turned off the lamp on the nightstand, lay down with a pillow over his face, and listened to the Doors.

"Fatigue," Phineas said. "Another sign."

Minutes later, Robby Krieger's guitar solo started. Gene followed it note by note, plucking an air guitar, so that he didn't hear Phineas talking about his days in Chile.

"I would get so terribly sleepy," Phineas said. "Rise at three a.m. Groom and feed the horses. Harness them to the coach. Depart at four in total darkness. Pitch black. Load luggage. Collect fares. Be polite to the *pasajeros*! *Muy cortés*. So polite over a hundred kilometers in roughly thirteen hours. Beautiful country, but those roads. Terrible compared to these carpets you drive on today. And that was all in the shadow of political instability. Even downright revolution. I really had to have my wits about me. It was foreign at first. The customs and language. But I learned. In spite of my injury. The animals, the routine …"

Phineas's voice faded into the background as Gene's mind drifted along with Robbie's solo, a riff off Coltrane's "My Favorite Things." This was a live version of "Light My Fire" he had never heard before.

Perhaps there was a faint similarity between the flashing circuitry of neurons in his recently traumatized brain and the smashed electronics in the garbage that should have been playing the following message:

> Gene? Are you there? It's Dave. Are you OK, man? Did you lose your cell phone? I've been trying to get in touch with you all week. Mainly because you lost the bet and I need you to open for the showcase. Kidding! Only kidding. Seriously, though. The hospital said that you just up and left without being discharged. I hope you're feeling better. I'm flying back from Denver tomorrow morning. Give me a call. Let me know you're OK. I've been worried about you, buddy. We all are. That was quite a blow to your ol' noggin. I've been thinking it should've been me. No kids or family. And I'm probably the one that really needs some sense knocked into my thick head. Let me know if there's anything I can do for you or your fam. Hope you're feeling better. And give me a call.

Monday, November 6th, 2017

At the Cross Creek Golf Course in Temecula, California, Gene got to the 6th tee and looked around. There was no one within three holes, in front or behind.

"This course and I have something in common," Phin said. "We both have fungus growing." Standing next to a mushroom growing on a grassy slope, he tilted his head to show a large mushroom flowering from his skull. The bow tie and jacket were gone. He wore his pants and undershirt and held the tamping iron like a hiking stick.

Gene removed his golf bag from the cart and took a water bottle from the basket.

"I guess Mr. Grumpy Pants over there is too busy," Phin said to the iron. "But Rod, I know you'll listen to me. My Constant Companion, always with me, like my sorrow." He started humming the tune to "I Am a Man of Constant Sorrow."

"Catchy song, isn't it, Rod?" Phin said. "Our new buddy Gene sure has some good music. Can't say I need to hear his "Fire" playlist again, but the right tune sure can comfort the heart. Did I ever tell you about the music in Chile? Accordions, guitars, drums. Then up in the mountains they had lovely instruments. No strings. All sorts of flutes and pipes. The trutruka, which is like a trumpet. Melodies from another world. I still remember them, like the wind. They give me chills. Haunting, truly haunting."

Gene unzipped a side pocket and pulled out a small case for sunglasses. He ran up a nearby hill and took a slow look around.

"I had a wada once," Phin said, "which is a pumpkin filled with pebbles. Basically a rattle. Whatta wada player I used to be."

Gene returned. He opened the case, removed a golf tee covered with match heads, and pushed the tee into the ground.

"He's not listening to me, Rod," Phin said, yanking the large mushroom from the ground by the base of its stalk. "He's lost his mind. No longer Gene. They'll say he went insane. Worse than me. I was just a drunkard and a lout, if I remember correctly." He took a nibble of the mushroom.

"'Pertinaciously obstinate,' I believe the railroad said. Or maybe Doc Harlow. That's quite a phrase, isn't it, Rod?" A bunny ran across the tee.

"An animal! The animal passions of a strong man with the intellectual capacity of a child, Doc Harlow said about me."

Gene pulled a film canister from his golf bag. He opened it and spread red-and-white powder in a circle below the tee. He took one more look around to make sure there was no ranger or beer girl watching and opened his water bottle full of gasoline. Then, from the tee in the ground to the nearby bushes on either side, he poured two thin trails of gas out of the water bottle.

"It's the pressure," Phin said, addressing Rod and taking a large bite of the mushroom. He chewed, tasted something funny, and spit it out, tossing the rest aside. "Pressure on the brain is not a good thing. Makes a man act funny." He grabbed the mushroom sprouting from the hole in his head by its base and began tugging. It resisted at first, then gradually came loose.

"Ah, that's better," he said, smelling the mushroom. "Phew! That *is* bad. 'Excessively fetid' is what Old Doc Harlow said, but 'fetid' might not even do it justice." Phin waved the air in front of his nostrils. "He sure was right about the drainage, though. Which is what we need to do to our friend Gene." He threw the offending fungus from his brain into the bushes.

Gene took two more large water bottles from the inside of his golf bag and, removing the cap from one, doused the bushes and surrounding ground. He gathered some small sticks and dead leaves and put a little pile on the gas-soaked ground, right next to the tee sticking up. Then he collected more kindling and set it aside with the bottles near his cart.

"He won't seek medical attention or reach out to his family," Phin said. "Not me. Went right to the doctor. 'Here's business enough for you,' I said. Then I ran straight to Mommy as soon as I could." He pulled a flask from his back pocket and took a long gulp. "Mommy! Mommy! Phinny has a boo-boo! A big owie!"

He took another swig. "Whiskey. Now there's another comfort. Let 'em say I was a drunk." He inserted his finger into the wound on the top of his head and pulled out a small glob of brain. "Gray matter. White matter. How does it all matter anyway, in the end?"

Phin walked over and, leaning down on the tamping iron, he scooped up some of the powder Gene had sprinkled on the ground. Rising, he rubbed his fingertips near his nose and dabbed them with his tongue.

"Ahhh," he said. "I thought there might be some sulfur and phosphorus in that. A drunk and a gambler, the two of us. Who do you like tonight, Rod, in this modern American football contest? Packers or Lions? The Packers quarterback has a broken collarbone. Detroit is the safe bet. But what's the line at? Genie, do you know the line tonight?"

Gene pulled out his oversized titanium driver. He put a ball on top of the adorned tee and took one last look around. There was nobody. He had the course to himself.

"What I'm thinking, Rod, is that we can use one of these holes with the flags. The diameter is greater, but they're not so different from a drill hole. Some powder. A fuse. We'll get some sand from one of the traps, tamp it down nice and tight. Then we'll come out and play this game called golf, with our friend Gene. I'll use you instead of the flag. I'll set you down in the hole and tend you, just like I see these golfers do. Tenderly, I will tend you, my sweet Rod. I'll ignore the rules and keep you in the hole! When he reaches in for his ball, give us a spark. I'll aim you right at his cheek, then you get in there and release the pressure. Drainage. That's what we need to set old Genie straight. What caused my ailment will cure his."

Phin took another long gulp from his flask. He vomited prodigiously. Small chunks of brain geysered out of his skull as he crouched over, retching.

Gene swung hard, a wicked slice that he pushed badly. But he made good contact. The spark from the clubhead ignited the gas-soaked grass around the tee. The kindling pile caught and the flame followed the gasoline path to the bushes on the right like something alive seeking cover. The advancing wave of heat lit the bush in an instant. Gene went to work fanning the flames, adding twigs and leaves from his reserve pile of kindling. From the second pile, he grabbed a larger branch and held it to the fire like a kid roasting a marshmallow at a campfire. Once it caught, he carried the burning leaves to the left side of the tee and dropped it on the ground. He ran back to his cart, and, picking up his last water bottle of gasoline, flicked out half of its contents to the fire on the right, which flared up like a fierce and angry animal. He poured the rest of his bottle on the left side of the tee, doubling the size of the small flames with an audible *whoosh* sound.

He looked around—still nobody. The front nine of this particular course was in the middle of nowhere. There were no houses or roads or anything, only some large estates in the distance. He was alone with the fire that was now spreading to the bushes on each side, the branches crackling and hissing. He watched it reach drought-ravaged chaparral and begin to grow.

It had worked. He wasn't sure that it would, but it had. It had worked perfectly. The fire grew and rose and raced forward along both sides of the fairway. How quickly it moved both astonished and frightened him. He also noticed that the fear was something he enjoyed, like the thrill of a roller coaster.

"All it takes is a spark, eh, Gene?" Phin said from his knees, wiping his mouth with his bare arm.

The flames transfixed Gene, for he was not seeing flames, but instead a large crowd of orange swirling faces: the audiences from improv theaters in Chicago and Los Angeles that he had failed to capture, an entire sea of bemused, bored, and indifferent expressions. As he continued to watch, the faces changed. The laughter began, first as a giggle. As the flames grew in size and intensity, so did the laughter that Gene imagined, until finally the laughing flames morphed into an uproar brought on by something hilariously funny—not just funny, but funny and true. He had reached them with a nugget of truth that the entire audience could relate to, profound and personal, that feeds on itself because it's just so darn funny. And it was Gene that had started it all. He stood in the fairway and basked in their laughter and applause until the heat singed his skin. Then he took off.

*

"Mom, I have another call I need to take," Nick said. "It's my boss. I'll call you tomorrow."

Nick switched over. "Hey, Nick, we got a fire over in Temecula," Alister said. "A golf course. Meet me at the Park-n-Ride in Escondido. How soon can you get there?"

"Depending on traffic, close to thirty minutes," he said.

"OK, see you there."

Nick went into the kitchen. Ashley was cooking. "I gotta go," he said. "There's a fire in Temecula."

"I'll make a plate for when you get back. How's your dad?"

"He's stable," Nick said. "They're still waiting on the CT scan to figure out what kind of stroke he had."

"Drive carefully. How's your headache?"

"It's not too bad today. Love you." He kissed her goodbye.

"Love you too."

*

Rosie O'Grady's Pub
Monday Night Football Week 9
Detroit Lions vs. Green Bay Packers

They sat on their usual barstools. The broadcasters were discussing the injury to quarterback Aaron Rodgers, but the bar patrons weren't listening. They had their own injury to discuss.

"And you still haven't heard from him?" Harris asked.

Dave shook his head.

"Poor Gene."

"I know," Dave said. "The police have deemed it a missing person case."

Mike walked in and high-fived his way down the line. "Any word on Gene?" he asked, pulling out his phone and sitting down.

"Nothing."

"He'll be OK," Mike said, patting Dave's shoulder. "Gene's a tough old bird."

Mike ordered a beer and started scanning emails. An uncomfortable silence settled in on the crew as commercials blared above them.

Finally, the silence was too much for Harris. "Sorry about your boy Watson," he said to Dave. "Done for the year."

"In practice," Dave said, shaking his head.

"What happened in practice?" Jimmy said, walking into Rosie O'Grady's. Jimmy, a hugger, hugged each person in turn.

"Didn't you hear?" Harris asked.

"No," Jimmy said, settling in. "Crazy week at work." Both Gene and Nick's seats, like missing tackles on an offensive line, remained vacant.

"A brain scientist's work is never done," Dave said. "Of course, a lot of that time he's just playing sudoku. But still, if he wants to understand the human brain, he's gotta, you know, like, get past level Easy."

"Just like Mikey over here," Harris said, pointing at Mike on his phone. "Putting musicians on cruise ships all over the world, around the clock. His job never stops."

Jimmy ordered a beer. Mike nodded without looking up from his phone. "Harris," Dave said, "as an orthodontist, you're the only one of us that actually works regular nine-to-five hours."

"Straightening teeth and straightening lives," Harris said, raising his bottle and taking a drink. "Hey, did you guys hear that Nick got both a new job *and* a new house?"

Dave and Jimmy both shook their heads. Mike was on his phone.

"Arson investigator," Harris said. "Started this week."

"That'll keep him busy," Dave said. "I should know—I used to investigate arses meself."

"I think he means arson, you know, like fire," Jimmy said with a goading smile.

"Oh, I know all about arses and fire, don't you worry your pretty little head," Dave said in a perfect Scottish accent, signaling Betsy the bartender for another beer. "William Wallace is seven feet tall and shoots fireballs out of his arse."

"Wait," Jimmy said. "What were you guys going to tell me? The crazy thing that happened."

"Nick is investigating arses," Dave said, flipping back to his regular voice like a switch. "He's probably got poo nose. That's a thing."

"No, not that," Jimmy said, holding back a smile. "Something that happened in practice."

"Oh, that," Harris said. "Houston's quarterback Deshaun Watson tore his ACL in practice this week, and Dave here is crying a river because he had him in fantasy."

"In practice?" Jimmy asked. The game kicked off on the screens all over the bar.

"In practice," Harris said. "Done for the year."

Dave slanted his Bears hat and became Allen Iverson. "If I can't practice, I can't practice, man. Simple as that."

The group laughed. Betsy brought over Dave's beer, and he directed his routine toward her. "We in here, talkin' about practice," Dave as Allen Iverson said. "I mean listen. We talkin' about practice."

Jimmy signaled for a beer and nodded at the empty stool. "Any word on Gene?"

Harris shook his head.

"I hope he's all right," Jimmy said.

"I mean, listen," Dave continued. "What are we talking about? Not the game that I go out and die for. How silly is that? Talkin' about practice."

The joke lost its steam. Rather than give it new life, Dave caught wind of Jimmy and Harris's conversation. "No, c'mon, Jimmy, you're the brain doc. How serious is hitting the left side of your head?"

Jimmy took a deep breath. "I don't know, I haven't examined him," he said, indicating the top left half of his skull. "It might not be that bad. Or … it might be bad. Language issues. Mood. Maybe he has complications with one side of his body or his face. Balance. Solving problems. Organizing tasks. A lot happens in that area. Hopefully, wherever he is, he's getting seen by someone that can determine the extent of his injury."

Betsy came over with Jimmy's beer, and Dave joked with her that he was still waiting on his protein shake.

Harris turned to Jimmy. "So how do you and Mike know each other?" he asked. "It's hard keeping track of all of you, being the newest Chicagoan to this group."

"We went to the same high school in Glenbrook, near Riverview where these guys are all from," Jimmy said. "Mike and I were close growing up, though we drifted apart when he first started singing on a cruise ship."

"Mike, you sang on a cruise ship? That's amazing!"

"It was fun."

"Well," Harris said, "I can't tell you how nice it's been to have found a group of Chicagoans to watch the Bears games with. It makes all the difference."

"It sure does," Jimmy said. "This is a passionate group. And you're from Galena? Right?"

"Actually, a small town near Galena. Hanover."

"And how did you end up with this group?" Jimmy asked.

"Nick was my old neighbor, before he met Ashley," Harris said. "These clowns used to come to Nick's for the games. I just got swallowed up into the group."

"Cheers," Jimmy said. "To the Bears."

"And to swallowing," Dave added.

Everyone cheered with bottle clinks. Mike went back to his phone. Betsy came over to shoot the bull with Dave. Jimmy leaned around Mike and shouted, "What are you talking about over there?"

"What are we talkin' about? We talkin' about practice."

On a third and six, a Detroit receiver dove and caught the ball, or did he? The ruling on the field was that he caught the ball, but the Green Bay coach challenged this decision by tossing a little red flag (that a zebra had to subsequently pick up). A replay of the fingertip grab was shown in slow motion from various angles. The patrons of Rosie O'Grady's Pub, as well as millions of people everywhere, offered up their opinions. The broadcast froze the action and replayed the catch again from different vantage points while a rules expert chimed in. Then the officials with ultimate say, people that get paid to sit in a room and cast judgements of established professional football rules to stadiums across the land (nice work if you can get it) phoned in on a direct line with their decision: the player didn't control the ball. The ruling on the field was overturned. The zebra handed back the little red flag to the Green Bay head coach, who stuffed it in his pocket with an air of defiance. The Detroit punting unit took the field and the escapism that is American professional football resumed for the 81,441 people at Lambeau Field, the millions of people watching around the world, and our fair patrons of Rosie O'Grady's Pub sitting alongside the ominously empty seat of Gene Santos.

Monday Night Football results Week 9
Detroit Lions 30 Green Bay Packers 17

*

Tuesday, November 7th, 2017

Nick woke up with a headache. There were texts on his phone from last night that he read but didn't respond to. He was trying to pull back the wisps of his dream, an elusive feeling of safety and happiness, of well-being. It was January 1986, he was in the Superdome in New Orleans at Super Bowl XX. His dad was there, wearing a Bears sweater vest, being carried away by all the Bears players … but where were they taking him? The feeling of euphoria, of victory, that permeated the dream vanished and instead the dream ended with a feeling of uncertainty and fear.

Ashley kissed him on the forehead. She told him to get in the shower, take his medicine, and have some coffee, then see how he feels. He went into the bathroom and looked at his reflection. His head was pounding. Out of nowhere he thought back to his childhood, when his father worked at a Chinese restaurant in a nearby shopping mall for a few years during the week to help make ends meet. Nick could a bring a friend and usually brought Gene to go visit and sit in the back where there was a one-way mirror. They could see the customers, but the customers could only see their own reflections. Behind the mirror, Gene and Nick would make faces at the customers that were none the wiser. It was a riot.

Nick stared at his reflection, and it felt like something was hiding behind it now, jeering and mocking him. He swallowed his medication and turned on the shower, watching as steam covered the mirror.

Growing up in Riverview, a northern suburb of Chicago, there were three things expected of Nick Moy: get straight A's, practice piano for one hour a day, and faithfully attend the Riverview Asian Christian Church every Sunday, where his father was a minister.

The first two requirements were not difficult for Nick. Grade school was not particularly challenging, and the piano would occasionally capture his imagination *and* competitive spirit, since he was also required to compete in regional youth piano competitions.

The church service, on the other hand, was excruciating right from the start. He had to sit in the front pew with his mother and older sister. Every Sunday it was the same—donuts for breakfast, then church until around two in the afternoon. As a young child, this meant Sunday school. Once Nick turned seven, though, he was expected to sit quietly, pay attention to the sermon, and be prepared for questions after the service. His father's sermons, for most of his childhood, clocked in at around two and a half hours on average.

The hardest part for young Nick, besides sitting still, was in the autumn when church forced him to miss roughly 80 percent of Chicago Bears football. When his beloved Bears kicked off at noon, as they usually did, there was an outside chance of catching the fourth quarter if it was a shorter sermon and both Nick and his sister, Julia, answered their father's questions satisfactorily.

Nick's developing piano success was a bridge connecting him and his father. It was the only thing that could keep his father from church on Sunday. When the Bears and a piano competition landed on the same day, it was as if a tremendous clash between father and son and religion and music and professional football jammed the bridge into gridlock. This confrontation reached its apex in January of 1986. Nick had his first national piano competition in Florida on the same day as Super Bowl XX, featuring the Chicago Bears and the New England Patriots. Nick, strong-willed and stubborn at the age of eight, agreed to compete only if his father brought along the Beta VCR and recorded the game. The morning following the competition, Nick watched the Bears thrash the Patriots. His father sat at the desk in the hotel room with classical music playing on Nick's Walkman, drafting next week's sermon. His father didn't turn around once in three hours as Nick jumped on the bed celebrating sacks and fumbles and touchdowns. In the corner by the suitcases, like a third presence in the room, a shiny and gratuitously large piano trophy gleamed.

"You played well yesterday, son," his father said, adjusting his headphones and turning as the triumphant Bears players carried coaches Ditka and Ryan off the field.

Monday, November 13th, 2017

Rosie O'Grady's Pub
Monday Night Football Week 10
Carolina Panthers vs. Miami Dolphins

"Anything from Genie?" Harris asked, plopping down and glancing at the empty seat.

"Nothing," Dave said. "His wife. The hospital. Police. Not a word. Only the five-hundred-dollar withdrawal from the ATM in Escondido."

They drank in silence for a moment as the Dolphins and Panthers kicked off Monday Night Football.

"Is Jimmy coming tonight?" Harris asked.

"I believe so," Dave said. "Don't you read your texts?"

"I don't think I'm on the text stream," Harris said.

"Well let me add you before you start spilling your period juice."

Harris laughed, spitting his beer. "Too late." He wiped his mouth with his sleeve. "Nick?"

"Nope," Dave replied. "Investigating arses. They've put him right to work. Like Mikey here." Mike looked up from his phone and smiled.

"There's been another case of arse— as in arson—today," Harris said. "On another golf course. Up in Riverside. Did you guys hear?"

"I notice everything about arses," Dave said. "If there's something to notice about an arse, I'm going to notice it."

Jimmy walked in and started in on his hugs.

"Like this arse here," Dave said, rising.

"See, doesn't that feel good, everyone?" Jimmy said.

"That was an ugly one yesterday," Dave said as they sat down at the bar and ordered a round. "I hate losing to the Packers."

"Have you ever seen anything like that challenge?" Harris asked.

Mike, not taking his eyes or thumbs off his phone, grunted. "What happened?" Jimmy asked. "I missed the game."

"Cunningham dove for the pylon and the refs ruled him out at the two," Dave explained as the beers arrived. "Fox challenged it, thinking that the ball had crossed the pylon for a tuddy. Instead, on review they determined that he lost control of the ball *before* he went out of bounds and *before* he touched the pylon, resulting in a touch-back for the Packers. I've never seen anything like it."

"Brutal," Harris said. "And they lost by seven. What are we now, three and six?"

"Season is over," Jimmy said. "Done-zo. Put it on ice."

"It's over now," Harris confirmed.

Mike, still not looking up from his phone, started singing "It Must Have Been Love."

Betsy the bartender came over. "Mike, karaoke is on Thursdays," she said. Mike ignored her, singing whole-note "aaaahhhh" harmonies.

"If you keep it up, I'm going to have to ask you to leave," Betsy said with her eyes smiling, only making Mike hit the next chorus with added gusto.

Harris turned to Jimmy. "Jimmy, is it true you used to work for the Bears?"

"True," Jimmy replied. "My dad was an ophthalmologist for the Bears. He's retired now."

"Ophthalmologist," Harris said. "I remember that's the word I missed in the finals of the spelling bee in sixth grade. Heck of a word to spell. I'll never forget that. Funny the way memory works."

Mike dodged a wet towel from Betsy, singing that it must have been love.

"I still remember Jimmy's license plate in high school said 'NFL OD,'" Dave said.

"Dave made fun of me for it because he thought it was an error, like it was supposed to be double zero," Jimmy added. "Jerk."

"I honestly didn't know," Dave said.

"Like hell you didn't," Jimmy said. "Yeah, my dad was the Bears' eye doctor."

Mike belted out the chorus again while Dave held up his phone's flashlight. Some Dolphins fans raised their hands and started swaying. Betsy was laughing. More cell phone lights came on in the bar.

"Can *this song* be over now?" Betsy jeered. Mike smiled as he sang.

"That's amazing you worked for the Bears," Harris said to Jimmy. "What did you do?"

"Please don't get him started," Dave said.

"Everything. Laundry. Equipment. Raising and lowering nets for field goals. Throwing balls in from the sideline. I can throw a mean underhand spiral," Jimmy said. Behind him, Dave shook his head to the contrary. Betsy threw a lemon at Mike, which he caught as he finished off the song to applause from the Dolphins fans.

"Isn't it something that all of us ended up out here in San Diego?" Harris said. "I just came because I was sick of winter. What about you, Jimmy?"

Jimmy told him about his residency, and the interview he'd had at UCSD for a position with the Junior Seau Foundation research faculty the weekend of Gene's wedding. Two baskets of chicken wings and sauces arrived.

"Anything new on Gene?" Betsy asked the group.

"Unfortunately not," Harris said. "He's disappeared without a trace. I really think we need to form a search party."

"Didn't his wife specifically ask us not to get involved with the search?" Jimmy asked.

"Actually," Dave said, "there is something a little weird. His clubs. Before I took Gene to the hospital, I threw his clubs in his car and gave him back his keys. The car stayed in the Twin Oaks parking lot until three days later when his wife Angela went with a neighbor to pick it up. They get home, and no clubs. They're gone. Now how do you explain that?"

Everyone shrugged.

"Stolen?" Betsy asked.

"No sign of a break-in," Dave said to a row of blank stares.

There was a long silence.

"For some reason I can't figure out," Dave said, "I think Gene went back for his clubs. But why would he get his clubs? It makes no sense."

The Panthers defense sacked the Dolphins quarterback, causing the ball to tumble loose for a fumble. Or did it? The zebras huddled together, first to pull bodies off a pile, next to discuss the ruling. The replay appeared on the screen, slipping into slow motion to show the quarterback's arm going forward. But when did the ball come loose? An expert joined the broadcast. The zebras broke the huddle and the head zebra announced the ruling on the field: a fumble recovered by the defense. The Dolphins coach tossed his little red flag high in the air and once again America's most popular form of escapism was on pause.

Monday Night Football results Week 10
Carolina Panthers 45 Miami Dolphins 21

*

"I'm not saying comedy isn't necessary," Phineas said to Gene from across the booth inside a Chick-fil-A. Once again, he wore his jacket and bow tie. He rubbed his hand slowly along the shaft of his tamping iron, examining the metal closely with both his fingertips and his good eye.

"Vital, more like," Gene said, biting into his chicken sandwich. "You sure you don't want some fries or something?"

"No, I'm not terribly hungry," Phineas said. "My appetite comes and goes."

"Suit yourself."

"It's just that I don't think these comedy performances offer the structure that you need," Phineas said.

"I've got all the structure I can handle," Gene said, sipping his shake.

"But there are things you need to relearn," Phineas said. "With the right care, a modest work schedule, you can reforge critical connections that you've lost. When I returned to New Hampshire—"

The Chick-fil-A cow came in from outside.

"C'mon, Phin," Gene said. "Did you hear the audience tonight? I've never felt so alive."

"Please, call me Phineas," he said, feeling the scar on his cheek. "But what about your wife and kids? Your friends? Your old life?"

"It'll be there," Gene said, nodding and acknowledging the waving cow. He held up his shake. "Your milk is delicious."

"But your old life," Phineas said, "is how you reestablish the original connections you've lost. With familiarity and basic structure you can build alternate pathways. Give the medical community a chance to help you. When I was in Chile—"

"Shut the hell up!" Gene yelled. "For the love of God, shut up about Chile! Shut up about structure! Shut the hell up about my family! Drop it! Leave it alone! Or else I'll shove your friend Rod so far up your ass it'll go right through your brain again."

Gene looked around the restaurant. Everyone stared, including the cow. He had somehow failed to notice that all the other patrons were NFL football players in full uniform. He saw Vikings, Browns, Chargers, Steelers, Chiefs, Saints, Raiders. But something was wrong. A Giant was trying over and over to push on the entrance door, even though it was a pull. A Patriot couldn't figure out the ketchup dispenser. A Buccaneer couldn't get the chicken sandwich past his face mask. A Titan couldn't get his straw in his shake. A fight erupted between a Cowboy and an Eagle.

Gene closed and rubbed his eyes. When he opened them again, the Chick-fil-A restaurant had transformed into a crowded nightclub. The comedian on stage was Bob McLauren. He had bandages wrapped around his head, and a crumpled bicycle lay at his feet. He was doing a routine about Frankenstein creating a profile on Match.com, yet his timing was off. The audience wasn't laughing. Gene surveyed a bizarre, chaotic scene. A boxer was shadowboxing, and losing. A woman in equestrian apparel sat backward on a chair and kept calling out, "Whoa!" A construction worker with a giant dent in his helmet kept asking no one in particular, "What is that, Gary, about a one-by-eight?" A woman in a swimsuit was singing, "Nightswimming, deserves a pool with water." There were kids crying, clutching their scooters and skateboards. A surfer was pretending that the floor was a board, but she kept losing her balance. A soccer player appeared to be heading an invisible ball over and over. A hockey player with a stick was running around celebrating an imaginary goal. A man covered in glass was steering an invisible wheel with one hand and texting with the other. A mustachioed, muscular, bald man wearing black leather was holding the handlebars of an imaginary motorcycle and kept saying, "Vroom, vroom." A peering baseball pitcher adamantly rejected an invisible catcher's signs over and over again. "Fine, but he's sitting on my heater," he said before going into his fastball wind-up.

One audience member in particular transfixed Gene. An old man in a natty, frayed robe with a giant purple bruise on his forehead cradled a sink. He stood solemn as a ghost in the middle of the chaos. His thin, hairless, skeletal legs embarked with small ragged-slipper steps, getting closer and closer to Gene. Once he was at the side of Gene and Phineas's table, he leaned down with wild, glittering eyes and spoke a poem with his toothless mouth.

> *I walked in the bathroom door*
> *My mind was able to think*
> *I slipped on the bathroom floor*
> *And hit my head on the sink.*

He paused, and a small puddle of drool collected on the table between Gene and Phineas.

> *I walked out the bathroom door*
> *My mind was not able to think*
> *Now I'm not me no more*
> *And my only friend is a sink.*

The man laughed a horrible, wheezy laugh. He hugged the sink and strolled back into the madness. "Oh, Sinky, my one and only," he said. Gene turned as, on stage, Bob McLauren kicked his busted bicycle and called out, "Will someone turn the lights down?"

The lights did seem unnecessarily bright. Gene closed his eyes and shook his head. "This is too much. Let's get out of here," he said.

*

Later, driving home, Gene turned down Van Halen's "On Fire" and said, "Look, Phin, I'm sorry. I didn't mean to snap at you back there. I just can't go back to my old life. It's not me. It's not who I am."

"It's who you were," Phineas said. "You were a good teacher. A father. A husband. You were happy. A decent person. And you can go back to that way of life. A life of purpose. I can't watch you throw it all away."

Gene stopped at a red light. Phineas turned to face him.

"Look," he said, "The railroad didn't take me back. No one says you have to go back to teaching. We can find something, anything, besides this comedy act. Maybe work with animals. Farming. Together we can do it. Find a routine. Get you well. Back to your family. Think of your children. We can find a way to live again."

The light turned green. Gene stared ahead and rubbed his temple.

"Maybe drive one of those oo-bur cars. Which reminds me. Did I ever tell you how I got back home to Lebanon, in New Hampshire? After the accident. When I left Vermont. I went in an enclosed carriage."

A car behind honked, and Gene stepped on the gas.

"It was padded," Phineas said. "The kind used for transporting the insane."

Friday, November 17th, 2017

Ashley and Nick had lived in their home in Ramona for one week. They moved in on Friday the 10th. The trouble started the next morning with a blunt clang on the roof at 6:15 a.m. Another one came at 6:32. And then again at 6:55. The abrupt clatters descended on their roof and patio with alarming frequency—nearly once an hour. It didn't take Nick long to figure out what it was. The evidence bounced all around their property—golf balls, followed by strange-shoed invaders. Their soft spikes made little crinkling sounds on the stone pavers as they walked in search of the white dimpled trespassers. Though Nick knew essentially nothing about golf or what the term "slice" meant, he realized with dismay that they were in a prime location for an errant tee shot to the right of the 6th tee.

During that first weekend, their house and yard were hit on average seven times a day. During the week, the average was around three solid strikes a day.

"I told you I never wanted to live on a golf course," Ashley said over another interrupted breakfast. They had argued over the move, with Nick winning. He wanted more property and a lawn, like he had growing up in Illinois. She wanted to live in North County, just north of San Diego, but in the end she agreed to live to the east because it was a bigger house.

Each sliced tee shot struck at the foundation of their new life together. Every day they were pelted, starting around six thirty or seven in the morning. After only a week, they already had a bucket full of balls. Ashley was working full-time as a medical assistant while studying for her nursing degree. She had worked the night shift that Thursday and came home exhausted and in no mood Friday morning when an errant drive smashed through the kitchen window and rattled around in the sink, settling in her recently deposited cereal bowl.

"I'll build a fence, maybe something with a net," Nick said. He was tired from driving out to Riverside all week to the latest golf course fire.

They laughed about it later that evening when he came in holding three white Styrofoam boxes of takeout from Ashley's favorite sushi restaurant.

"It's not just me you'll be protecting with that net," Ashley said. "And you're going to have to eat all that sushi yourself. Because I'm pregnant. Looks like your sperm pills worked after all."

Luckily, none of the sushi spilled when boxes hit the floor.

Tuesday, November 21st, 2017

Gene's playlist had grown. Hendrix's "House Burning Down," Billy Joel's "We Didn't Start the Fire," Stevie Wonder's "To Feel the Fire," and (requested by Phineas) "Dynamite" by Brenda Lee. Each Monday, he visited a new course in Southern California. After Temecula, he went north to Riverside, then back south and east to Ramona. Each time he made sure he was alone on the course at twilight. Then he set the 6th hole on fire using the same method: a tee with match heads, pyrotechnic powder, gasoline, and a titanium driver for the spark.

His first fire in Temecula burned twelve holes of the Cross Creek Golf Course, another 500 acres, and a couple of estates. His fire in Riverside County, at the Dos Lagos Golf Course in Corona, burned a similar acreage, three holes, and forced the evacuation of twenty homes in the golf course community that was less than a year old.

The Steele Canyon Fire, coinciding with Santa Ana wind conditions, was the biggest. He burned the entire Steele Canyon Golf Course, an additional twenty square miles in Jamul, and two dozen homes. There were no fatalities, but a man defending his home with a hose was badly burned.

After the first fire, the Temecula police and fire departments created a profile based on the vague "tall, thin, wearing a golf hat" description from the eighty-three-year-old starter that afternoon. After the Dos Lagos Fire, the alert was sent out to every golf course in every state in the western United States considered at risk for fire. After the Steele Canyon Fire, he became known as the Links Lighter and made national news. Cal Fire, with resources spread thin and Southern California reeling from its fifth straight year of drought, put all golf courses on high alert.

For Gene, each fire progressed in the same way. The faces of his audience appeared at first annoyed, bored, even despondent. Gradually the frowns turned. They became neutral, flickered, and then erupted into dancing flames of laughter—the greatest medicine—rioting into the sky. And Gene was the medicine man, the source of the healing. He was the one bringing light and laughter into the lives of the faces in the flames. He was the one the faces were quoting in their break rooms. As the fires were getting bigger, he was getting more and more famous. His stand-up was selling out. He was on the *Tonight Show*. He was in a movie. He had a Netflix special. He was the host of *Saturday Night Live*. As the fires consumed parched grass, dead trees, and dried brush, so the faces of his audience consumed his comedy. They couldn't get enough. Neither could he.

*

Gene started to have a recurring dream. In it, he is doing stand-up at a jam-packed club. He is in complete control. Slaying. It's easy. He knows the material like the back of his hand. His timing is impeccable. He is relaxed, at home in the spotlight, floating in laughter like it's warm water. These are his people.

Then something happens in the front row. A commotion of some kind. Someone has spilled a drink or choked on an ice cube or had some incident that draws attention. During the brief lull, Gene becomes aware that inches from his face is not a microphone, but in fact he is speaking into an oversized driver.

No one seems to be aware of this oddity. There don't appear to be any issues with acoustics or feedback or anything technical like that. The incident in the front row, whatever it is, gets resolved and Gene steps back into the groove. He is telling jokes he has told a thousand times. Guaranteed laughter, like pulling a string. He could do this routine in his sleep. Wait. He has that feeling, that semi-awareness in the middle of a dream. But he's not sure. The oversized driver-turned-microphone suggests that he is dreaming. But the stage, the audience, the lights, his own line of thinking … It all feels so real. Doubt creeps into his mind.

Dreaming or not, the show must go on. The doubt throws him off just a little, with his words and his timing and his delivery. If his jokes are drives, he is still hitting the fairway, but now there is a little fade, a slight pull. Little misses that he doesn't intend.

He takes a break to drink some water when he notices a conversation happening on the side of the stage. There is a large man in a suit with slicked-back hair having a discussion with the owner of the comedy club. Gene leans his ear in the general direction of the conversation, but the audience is calling out, howling, beckoning him back to the oversized driver-microphone.

Gene steps up and pulls a joke way out of bounds. Crickets. Pins drop. A cough. Gene hears the conversation on the side of the stage, and it's clear the man in the suit is from a golf association—either the USGA or the PGA or the PG of A or some amalgamation that ends in GA that means golf association. The driver that Gene is using for his microphone is the issue. It's not regulation, the man is saying. They see him watching them.

That's when the two men step up onto the stage. The man with the slicked-back hair inspects the driver. Gene sees that the skin on his neck is white and fleshy, like the belly of a fish. The audience is growing restless. The man pulls a measuring tape across the face of the driver with the comedy club owner looking anxiously on. The owner pulls out a bag of clubs and offers Gene a three wood. Gene tries to make a joke out of the matter. He declines the wood and asks for a 60 degree wedge—about as far from a three wood as you can get—but the owner is dead serious. He has fear in his eyes, so Gene accepts the next club he offers, a rescue four iron.

The owner somehow removes the oversized driver and attaches the rescue club to the microphone stand. Gene steps into the spotlight and grabs his new mic. But he fumbles and drops it. It clatters on the stage and Gene is frozen. He is not sure if he can pick up the club, or if it is like a ball in a sand trap and now the microphone/club has been grounded and there is some type of penalty he must declare. He looks to the man in the suit with the slicked-back hair for a ruling. The man is whispering in a hushed voice to the comedy club owner, presumably about the dropped club. It's not just his skin that is fishy and grotesque. He has strabismic, fishy eyes. The penalty must be very severe, indeed.

The audience makes for the exits. The man with the sickly pale glistening face approaches Gene, and now he can clearly see that this man is not from a golf association at all—he is an undertaker. As he begins measuring Gene for a coffin, Gene gets a whiff of his glistening skin. He reeks of fish.

In a flash, Gene is no longer in the comedy club, but standing on a putting green in broad daylight. It might be Torrey Pines, because he can hear the ocean. The crashing waves bring the sound of distant laughter. Gene is lining up a six-footer. The faces of the other players are hidden, but by their body language it's obvious a lot is riding on the putt. A hushed gallery watches intently.

Gene stands behind the ball. It's an uphill putt, with just a touch of left-to-right break. He can see the line. He does a practice swing, looks from his ball to the hole, back to his ball, and back to the hole once more to pick out the precise spot he wants to drill this putt.

That's when he sees that he's not putting into a hole at all. He's not at Torrey Pines or even on a golf course. He's in a graveyard, surrounded by mourners, six feet from his own grave. That's when he wakes up.

Wednesday, November 22nd, 2017

At the kitchen table, Nick swallowed a pill with his morning coffee and rested his head in his hands. Once his headache pain eased a bit, he opened his eyes and stared at the tile floor. A golf ball clattered on the roof. Fortunately, Ashley had gone to work twenty minutes ago, or else he would hear about the net he had yet to build.

Over the past few days, he had begun to think what life would be like as a father. He thought of the first time he had disappointed his own dad. It was his first C, in 1987, when he was in fifth grade.

Nick sat in the kitchen sipping his coffee, but in his memory he was far away, a child that wanted to please his father …

He got the C in PE for not getting dressed on time on ten different occasions during the quarter. The result: His father refused to allow him to watch the NFC Divisional Playoff. When the Bears lost to the Washington Redskins, which also happened to be Walter Payton's last game, Nick refused to play piano for a week. The standoff intensified before his mom was finally able to patch things up somewhat. Nick held the grudge for the rest of the winter.

As the '90s got underway, Nick started middle school and began to seriously challenge two of his parents' three expectations. His grades began to slip from As and Bs to Bs and Cs. This, and he battled with his father on a daily basis over the piano. His father rose to the occasion and used every carrot-and-stick method he could think of to keep his accomplished son playing the piano, hoping to fill up the newly built top shelf added to the crowded trophy case.

Nick's entire social life hinged on him practicing piano. This kept Nick playing, sort of, but only enough to see his friends on the weekends. So, like the Bears failing to advance past the divisional round,

Nick added no more trophies during those years, leaving the top shelf vacant.

Then in 1992, two dramatic events happened: The Bears fired Mike Ditka after going 5–11, and Nick quit playing piano. Nothing his father said or did mattered. Not even the big dangling carrot of a driver's license and the ability to share the car with his sister, Julia, could coerce him into ten minutes of scales on the ivories. Nick was burned out. His grades throughout his four years of high school also seemed to be strangely aligned with the mediocrity of the Dave Wannstedt–coached Chicago Bears; he mostly brought home Cs with a few Bs sprinkled in. His report card was just like any NFL team's 9–7 record. Average, but nowhere near good enough to please the fan base or, in this case, the parents nervously awaiting results.

Yet all through his upbringing—the highs and lows, the piano successes and failures, from the Super Bowl Shuffle all through the slow and steady decline of his beloved Chicago Bears—the third expectation remained, unflinching and implacable. He went to church every Sunday and sat in the front row with his mother and his sister.

And for a long moment, Nick was there, in between his mom and sister, his father's voice carrying, except he wasn't. He was sitting in the kitchen with a headache and a cold cup of coffee.

Saturday, November 25th, 2017

"Nick, what's wrong?" Ashley said. "You haven't said a word since we left my parents' house."

That morning, Ashley had gotten up and studied while Nick had gone to Home Depot to buy a new kitchen window and supplies to build a fence and a net to protect the house from golf balls. When he got home, he replaced the window and started on the fence, but then a migraine came on and forced him to lie down. His head was still hurting when they had to leave for Ashley's parents' house for an after-Thanksgiving dinner since they couldn't enjoy a meal on the real Thanksgiving due to Ashley's work schedule.

Now, Nick was driving south on the Five in gridlock traffic. To the west, the sun was setting into the Pacific. Despite Nick's shades, the sunlight hurt his eyes. To the east were the vast open hills of Camp Pendleton, the Marine Corps's major West Coast base. They inched along to Creedence Clearwater Revival's "Long as I Can See the Light."

Ashley turned the volume down.

"Nick, talk to me. What's wrong?"

"Nothing."

"Nick. Something is wrong. Is it your headaches? Did you call your neurologist?"

"I left a message," Nick replied. "You know how busy that place gets."

"Call them again," Ashley said. "Or call Jimmy. Talk to *someone*. You've been withdrawn lately. Sullen. I don't like it. You haven't said a word the whole drive. Everything at dinner was a one-word answer. My parents think you hate them."

"Just tired."

"Nick."

"I don't want to talk about it."

"Is your headache bad right now?"

"Not really."

"Is it your dad?"

"No."

"The baby?"

"No."

"New job?"

"No."

"The house? The stupid golf balls? *What* is bothering you?"

Nick looked out at all the red brake lights, the sunset over the ocean, the green hills. An Osprey helicopter flew low overhead. He watched the military aircraft. It felt like two dozen fingertips were pressing on his skull.

"Nick, talk to me. We can work through whatever's bothering you."

Nick watched the propellers go from vertical to horizontal as the helicopter landed in a field.

"Nick."

"I don't know, I guess I just feel …" he paused. "Lost."

"Lost? What are you talking about?"

"Lost and old. I feel old. We're old."

"Thirty-nine is not old."

They crawled along. Ashley's phone vibrated. She glanced down to see a GIF of a turkey holding a "Happy Turkey Day" sign from her friend Gabi. On low volume, the song "Lookin' Out My Backdoor" started. Ashley turned it off.

"Nick."

He sighed. "You know, there's another Creedence song. It's called 'Someday Never Comes.'"

"What?"

"'Someday Never Comes.' It's a song. I guess I just feel like …" He trailed off.

He took a breath and continued. "Like what I really want to happen never will."

"What do you really want to happen?"

"I don't know. There's this feeling I had when I was a kid. I had just won this big piano competition, the Bears had won the Super Bowl, my Dad and I were together. . . I guess I've been chasing that feeling my whole life. Triumph. That I was a winner. Or like that feeling of spring, renewal. I don't know what I'm saying— I guess I'm just depressed. We don't really talk that much. We're both always working, and when you're not working, you're studying. Sometimes it's like we don't even know each other. And now we're having a kid. We're having a kid. I mean, we just got married."

Ashley started crying. Her phone vibrated again. Gabi had sent another GIF. It said "Juice Boxes!" and showed a sitcom character holding up two large boxes of wine.

"Don't cry," Nick said. "It's my fault. I've always been this way. I've always been a little lost. Or broken. Or whatever. I don't know where it comes from. Like the headaches. It's mysterious."

Ashley was crying and looked out the window. They inched along.

"You could have told me you felt this way before I got pregnant." She took some tissue out of her purse and wiped her eyes.

Nick eased off the brake and coasted.

"I don't know how to talk about it. I kept thinking if I met the right girl, if I got a good job, the broken feeling, the lost feeling, would go away. Now I have all those things and the feeling is worse than ever."

Ashley wiped her eyes. "I'm very hormonal right now," she said. Her phone vibrated. Then vibrated again. She looked down at two more texts from Gabi. The first was a GIF of Snow White dancing with strobe lights. It said "I'VE BEEN DRINKING I'VE BEEN DRANKING." The second GIF was Jennifer Aniston dancing, arms extended, hair over her face, with the flashing words "#WHITEGIRLWASTED."

Ashley muted her phone and put it down.

"Nick, you better get your head out of your ass and figure it out. I'm not about to have this kid by myself."

Sunday, November 26th, 2017

Early Sunday morning, Ashley went out to study. Nick was about to get to work on the net when he decided instead to go to Harris's to watch the Chicago Bears get thrashed by the Philadelphia Eagles 31–3. He didn't respond to any of Ashley's texts and walked in the door at nine thirty that night, drunk as a skunk.

"Nick, did you drive home?"

"I'm fine. Jussa coupla drinks with the old Harris Wheel. Round and round with good old Harris Wheel."

"Nick, this isn't funny. You're wasted. And you drove."

"I'm a good drunk driver. I'm good at drunk driving. Speaking of being good at things. The Bears are not good at football."

"I don't give a fuck about the Bears!" Ashley screamed. "You could kill yourself, or someone else. Or get a DUI! What are you thinking?"

"I'm trying not to think too much these days, babe," Nick said. He burped, and a little vomit leaked out of the side of his mouth.

"Oh Jesus," Ashley said.

He stumbled past her into the bathroom. Later, she stepped around his passed-out body to get her toothbrush. She went into the kitchen to brush her teeth and kicked something with her foot. It was another golf ball. She looked up to see splintered cracks spiderwebbing away from a perfectly round hole in the brand new kitchen window.

Monday, November 27th, 2017

Nick was still asleep when Ashley left early the next morning. Normally, the sounds of her getting ready for her medical assistant job at seven a.m. woke him and he would start to get ready for work. But he didn't hear the shower, or her putting on makeup, or the beep of the coffee pot, or the loud slam of the front door.

The sound that did wake him up was the sound of her crying out because of a golf ball that traveled 215 yards before slamming into her slightly swollen stomach, knocking her to the ground, her to-go coffee mug hitting the pavement and spilling like tawny blood.

*

Rosie O'Grady's Pub
Monday Night Football Week 12
Baltimore Ravens vs. Houston Texans

"Did you guys have a good Thanksgiving?" Betsy said, setting down the beers.

Mike, Jimmy, and Harris all nodded from their new positions at the bar. Three Ravens fans sat on the end, like players lined up on the wrong side of the ball. Gene's stool was still empty.

"Where's the rest of the crew?" Betsy asked.

Jimmy answered for the group. "Dave is doing stand-up in Vegas. Nick is in town, he's just busy. New job. New house. Married. Excuses, excuses."

Betsy laughed politely.

"Weak, right? Where's the commitment?" Harris asked. Mike had to take a call.

"And still no word from Gene?" Betsy said, avoiding eye contact with the vacant seat.

"It's not good," Harris said. "He's been missing almost a month now. No one has seen him or talked to him or had any contact. Vanished. It's crazy—a missing person case. Gene's wife is relying on the police. We've offered to help, but we don't really know how."

"Well, I hope he's OK," Betsy said. A Ravens fan at the end of the bar, wearing an old Ray Lewis jersey, signaled her.

"Wait, talk slower. What happened?" Mike said into his phone.

"It's probably just as well that we didn't get together for the Bears game yesterday," Harris said.

"Did you watch it?" Jimmy asked.

"Unfortunately, yes," Harris responded. "Nick came over. It was ugly right from the start."

"Ugly ugly ugly," Jimmy said. "At 3–8 our playoff hopes are pretty much extinguished. How's Nick doing? Has his dad recovered from the stroke?"

"His dad is stable, but he's lost the ability to speak," Harris said.

Jimmy winced. "Strokes are all about time," he said. "Every second is crucial."

"OK, let me get this straight," Mike said into his phone. "You need a new drummer for the *Jersey Boys* show because the old one is in a holding cell for doing … what?"

"Nick was telling me English is his father's second language," Harris said, "and basically he just repeats the same Chinese curse word over and over again."

"Say that again," Mike said into his phone. Then he repeated what he heard in disbelief. "The smoke detector was activated by a burning undergarment."

The Ravens scored a tuddy. The end of the bar started to cheer and high-five.

"What word does he say?" Jimmy asked Harris.

"I guess it sounds like *gun dan*. The literal translation is rolling egg, or boiling egg, or something like that. But it means fuck off."

"How many crew members did you say had to go to the hospital for smoke inhalation?" Mike asked. "And you want our insurance to pay for it? I see. Wonderful."

"He just lies in bed and says 'fuck off' all day long," Harris said. "Nick's mom is a nurse and looks after him part of the time. They've hired someone too."

"That's rough," Jimmy said. "And Nick, how is he handling it?"

"Not good. Something is off with him," Harris said. "I couldn't put my finger on it exactly. I think his headaches are back. And then we ended up getting smashed."

"I should check in on him," Jimmy said. "He might need his meds adjusted."

Mike hung up the phone. "Everything's fine. Just a brief fire on a cruise ship."

Jimmy and Harris looked at him.

"I mean that literally," Mike said. "A brief fire. As in underwear."

They laughed. Jimmy's phone buzzed, and he looked down at the Cal Fire alert. "Didn't Nick move to Ramona?"

"Yeah, why?" Harris asked.

Jimmy showed him the alert.

On the screen the touchdown was under review. Did the ball cross the goal line before the player's knee touched the ground? The inches and milliseconds were under review, scrutinized in slow motion from various angels, awaiting judgement from the zebras.

Monday Night Football results Week 12
Baltimore Ravens 23 Houston Texans 16

*

The destruction of wildfires never ceased to amaze Nick. He always felt like he was walking on the surface of some distant moon or dead planet: the charred, smoking black ground, the bare, gnarled, scorched trees left behind, the absence of any sign of life amongst the burned remains. It filled him with both dread and awe.

That morning, Ashley had peeled out of the driveway before he had stumbled outside, bleary and hungover, wondering what had made her spill her coffee. She drove herself to the hospital before he even knew what had happened. In the afternoon she left him a voicemail telling him that a golf ball had hit her but giving no further details. Only the bare facts and a curt "Get some help. Whatever the problem is. Get help."

He was stuck in traffic, returning from Lakeside, the fingers on his skull tapping, tapping. Someone had left a lit stogie in a garbage can at the Willowbrook Country Club and the entire county freaked out. He was just finishing up his report when the Ramona fire broke out. By the time he made it home, there was no home left.

This time, the awe and wonder at the destructive capabilities of fire mixed with a raw, profound, and indignant feeling of loss. Three days before, he had a new house, a new wife, and a new child on the way. He regarded the smoldering ashes at his feet as some kind of mystic confirmation. It had all vanished, up in smoke, gone with the wind.

A pattern had emerged: It was always a Monday night and it was always the 6th hole. Nick gathered soil for the forensics team. He walked the still-smoking, blackened ground looking for other signs of evidence. So far, they had nothing on the Links Lighter but chemical traces suggesting a pyrotechnic powder.

His boss, Alister, called him.

"No, nothing so far," Nick said. The sound of his own voice was hollow.

"You're welcome to stay at my place," Alister said. "But you're welcome to get a hotel room if you just want to be alone without kids jumping all over you. For the time being, while you deal with the insurance. Use the company card for some clothes and whatever else you need."

Nick heard the flat, hollow sound of his own voice again. He popped another pill and kept walking. "Thanks boss," he said.

*

"Watch some more television," Gene said. "Your favorite pastime. Just watch. And for the love of God, stop talking." Gene clicked it on as Dorothy was meeting the Scarecrow. Phin watched the TV eagerly, while Gene went to work grinding another phone with his mortar and pestle.

"That's the trouble," the Scarecrow said. "I haven't got a brain."

"Did you hear that, Rod? This fellow doesn't have a brain."

Phin sat glued to the screen until the sound of smashed cell phone parts landing in the wastebasket roused him.

"You've got to be careful, Genie Boy," Phin said without taking his eyes off the screen. "Another ranger saw you yesterday. Another description. So what if it's not accurate, like what they said about me. Disfigured." He flashed a smile at the mirror and began rubbing his free hand on the tight, smooth, white canvas skull cap he wore. "Yet still a lady magnet." His hand moved from the back of his skull to the string tied tightly under his jaw. After learning about bacteria, he had convinced Gene to buy him the cap to protect his wound, despite Gene's claim that the cap would offer little. He tugged on the string while he stretched his jaw into a yawn. "Damn this thing!" He leapt up, untied the string, and flung the cap aside. "Why does it have to itch so?" He scratched the top of his head and tucked his undershirt into his pants. His jacket, tie, and shirt were on the back of a chair that he presently leaned his tamping iron against. "The three of us should all go out tonight," Phin said, once again rapt by the flashing images. "Chase some tail. Maybe hit a casino. TJ is just across the border."

From the mortar, Gene poured bits of ground cell phone into the wastebasket. Some of the smaller pieces landed on the floor. "Sonovabitch," he said, bending down to pick them up.

The word grabbed Phin's attention momentarily. He sat down and turned back to the screen. "You've been on the run for almost a month. You're wife. She's probably worried sick. Making calls. News reports. People are on the lookout. Friends. Police. The fire department. You've left quite a trail for people to follow. This Ramona fire burned a lot of homes. You're lucky you haven't killed anyone. Just a few animals." He reached over with his foot and slid the skull cap across the floor toward him. He picked it up and put it back on. "I'm sure Doc Harlow would be pleased to see me taking precautions—I can't stomach the thought of another infection," he said, pulling the string tight under his chin. "I never had a wife or children." He stood and approached the TV. When Dorothy reappeared on the screen, he pressed the back of his hand to her cheek. "I always wanted a family. But after the accident, for some reason the ladies didn't go for the guy with ptosis. Want to feel my sphenoid bone?" he asked Dorothy. "What's a matter, never seen a man's zygomatic arch?"

Gene picked up his new phone, which was attached to the charger in the wall, and scrolled with his index finger. He sat down on the edge of the other bed.

Phin stood nearby and regarded him. "Nothing? C'mon, Gene, that's funny! Suggesting that my droopy eyelid is a desirable sexual trait. Comparing an arch in my inner skull to a man's genitals. You of all people should be able to see the humor there." Phin turned to his tamping iron. "You think it's funny, don't cha, Rod?" His attention went back to the screen as Dorothy applied oil to the rusted Tin Man. "I sure wouldn't abandon my family if I had one though. My mother and uncle came straight from New Hampshire. It was a great comfort to have them there during the recovery."

Gene leaned back on the bed and closed his eyes. He moaned softly, rubbing his temple.

Phin sat back down at the TV and watched, mesmerized. "Did you hear that, Rod? This one doesn't have a heart."

The scene ended. He looked over at Gene, then turned and said to his iron, "Did you know that until about 1500, the predominant view was that the heart, not the brain, exercised psychological functions like thinking and feeling?"

Gene opened his eyes, sat up, and began scrolling on his phone again.

"Aristotle emphasized the heart," Phin said, crossing his legs, "while Hippocrates emphasized the brain. The majority believed Aristotle." He picked up his flask, tipped his head back, and swallowed the last few drops. "So much for majorities."

Phin reached over and waved his hand in between Gene's eyes and his phone.

"Just too much pressure on the brain," he said. "It's what I've been saying all along, Rod. We've got to find a way to release it, to help our friend Gene out. Now where's that bottle of whiskey hiding?"

*

Nick turned the lights off and lay in the dark, trying in vain to find a comfortable arrangement of the pillows on his uncomfortable hotel bed. His head pounded. He was simultaneously exhausted and wide awake. He recalled, for the ten thousandth time, the moment in his view when things began to go wrong …

A curious phenomenon arose in 1992, coinciding with the arrival of Brett Favre and (for Nick) the agonizing domination of the Green Bay Packers over the Bears: His father began to have car accidents. From 1992 until 1999, when the Bears went 3–13 against Green Bay (including an unfathomable ten-game losing streak from 1994 to 1998), his father had one car accident a year. Each successive accident wracked him further physically, and there was a corresponding decline in his mental health.

His father was never a particularly good driver, yet in the same manner Bears coach Dave Wannstedt might respond to the Atlanta Falcons trading Favre to the Packers, he claimed all of the accidents were outside of his control.

"My life is in God's hands," his father would say after each accident.

The first accident, in April of 1992, was the only one in which he wasn't alone. The day the Bears drafted defensive end Alonzo Spellman in the first round, Nick was in the passenger seat of the family Saab without his seatbelt fastened. The two of them were on their way home from picking up donuts early one Sunday morning when they came around a corner and nearly hit a deer. His father swerved and plowed head-on into a tree. Nick went flying into the windshield, leaving behind a hairline crack. He was small for his age, prepubescent, and it was the first time his mother felt that his size was a blessing.

That day, Nick missed church for only the second time in his childhood, the first being when he had the measles. His mom had heard the crash from the kitchen—they were only a few blocks from home. She handled it all calmly, in nurse mode, familiar with emergencies. She called a tow truck, jumped in the other family car (also a Saab), and dropped Nick's father off at church on the way to the hospital.

The doctors diagnosed Nick with a concussion. In the months afterward, he suffered from sporadic headaches. His mom took him to a neurologist and a headache specialist. The CT scan came back inconclusive. They prescribed Tylenol and rest.

After his father's second accident, a rear-end collision that wrecked his new Saab, he began to get headaches just like Nick. The focus of his sermons started to slip. He would repeat himself, or lose his train of thought, or go on tangents from his tangents and not be able to find his way back. The large and faithful congregation collectively and covertly denied that anything was wrong. Instead, they just daydreamed more than usual.

"My life is in God's hands."

His father's third accident was in 1994, when he got T-boned by a Toyota Corolla that ran a red light. His left arm was completely smashed and in a cast and sling for close to six months, and his sermons began to push four hours in length. They essentially became long, rambling religious tirades. Attendance, unlike at Soldier Field, suffered. There remained a loyal and dedicated following of faithful die hards. They felt that abandoning their minister during his health trials would be akin to abandoning their God.

"My life is in God's hands."

*

After the fourth accident—a nasty head-on collision with a drunken teenager right down on Duffy Lane, a two-lane street a mile from their house in Riverview with a high speed limit and a straightaway teens used for racing—his father began to wrap his own head in bandages each morning, claiming that they helped his headaches. His father seemed to have lost the ability to control the volume of his voice, at times speaking exceptionally loud, other times in a barely audible whisper. Nick's mother implored him to see Nick's neurologist, but he refused medical care, preferring the tightly wrapped bandages and alternately chewing mung beans, ginger, garlic cloves, and ginkgo leaves. Next to his Bible and notepad was always a repugnant napkin full of chewed-up stuff that made Nick cringe. Nick's mom would offer his dad an empty bottle or a cup, but he was stubborn about that too.

"My life is in God's hands."

After the fifth accident, in 1997, his father needed a hip replacement, and his pronunciation suffered. The volume issues shifted toward too loud. He began to have fits of stuttering.

"Dad, let me drive you today," Nick said.

"Why? My life is in God's hands."

The sixth accident, in 1998 (and the third time being rear-ended), wrecked his father's already ravaged spine. Following that accident, he wore the head bandages, a full back brace, a neck brace, and a sling on his left arm. He preached next to the pulpit from a wheelchair. It was during this year that Nick's father's sermons went from no theme or clarity to a singular focus: the fires of Hell.

For the final twelve months of Nick's Sunday attendance—fifty-two different sermons that railed over three hours—his father ranted and raved, pleaded, screamed, extolled, pondered, and beseeched the dwindling congregation about the burning fires of Hell in a way that even Dante would find excessive. The remaining handful of die-hard faithfuls would listen politely for the first hour before quietly and unassumingly heading for the exits, much like Bears fans during the fourth quarter in a game already decided.

1998 was the last year that Nick would attend the Sunday services at the Riverview Asian Christian Church, as he had enough credits from his second year of community college to achieve his long-sought goal of leaving home.

The next year things went from so-so to bad for Chicago Bears fans with the death of Walter Payton. Nick followed suit. He grew his hair out and dyed it orange. He started drinking and doing drugs—in the morning. He listened exclusively to Pink Floyd. He did just enough work to pass his classes and not move home. The Bears hired Dick Jauron and didn't fare much better.

On the morning of March 10th, 1998, Nick sat reading a newspaper article about Mike Singletary talking Alonzo Spellman down from a standoff with a SWAT team the day before. Suddenly the words turned bleary and he couldn't focus. That afternoon, Nick went to see his neurologist. It was his first diagnosed migraine.

*

Gene picked up the remote. "I'm going to play some music while I work," he said, putting the Cowardly Lion on mute. The new playlist started with Jerry Lee Lewis's "Great Balls of Fire." He stood and went over to the desk to prepare his tees.

Phin belched and returned his gaze to *The Wizard of Oz*. When Adele's "Set Fire to the Rain" started, he said, "Must every song we listen to have fire in it?"

Gene ignored him.

"No more fire music no more fire music no more fire music no more—"

Gene picked up his phone and switched it to Pink Floyd's *Dark Side of the Moon*.

Soon Dorothy and company could see the Emerald City in the distance, just as the song "Time" came from Gene's phone. Phin barely blinked as Dorothy fell in a field of flowers. Gene continued working deliberately.

The song "Great Gig in the Sky" started. Dorothy reached the Guardian of the Gates. Phin watched with rapt attention as Dorothy and her friends went inside the Emerald City. He scratched first his groin and then the canvas skull cap. "Why does the horse change color?" he asked, petting his tamping iron on his lap as if it were a small furry animal. "This invention, this television, is so very strange."

Gene blew on his finished tees. He looked on with Phin as the Wicked Witch wrote with her broom "SURRENDER DOROTHY" in the sky. He blew once more on the tees for good measure and walked over to put them in his golf bag.

Phin worked his bound jaw. "Damn! It's just so itchy!" He untied the string and threw the cap again.

By the bed, Gene bent down, unzipped the black canvas bag, and began counting his money.

Phin's eyes darted back and forth from the screen to Gene spreading the bills on the floor.

"Running a little low on funds? Another reason to hit a casino. We can double that in an hour," Phin said with a grin. He stood, leaned the tamping iron against the wall, and snatched up his flask. Hovering over Gene, who was on his knees, Phin unscrewed the flask and glugged a few swallows. The opening to the song "Money" startled him. "Is this even music?" He tossed the flask on the bed and kicked his skull cap.

"Doctor's orders," Phin scoffed, pacing in front of the desk. "You should see a doctor, Gene, but you know not all of them are going to be looking out for your best interest. Some of them might even be after your head." He rubbed his grinning jaw and bent down to whisper in Gene's ear. "Or your brain." Phin put a foot on the bed, pulled up a pant leg, and started itching his calf. "It's so dry here in Southern California. Doesn't it ever rain?"

Gene was recounting the bills.

"Take that doctor," Phin said, searching the ceiling. Then, as if a crack contained the answer, "Bigelow! That was his name. He was a bad seed all right." Phin pulled his second pant leg up and started scratching the other leg. "Did I tell you that he brought me to Boston? On his own dime. To show me off. Like a little pet." His voice changed to a high-pitched singsong. "The Boston Society for Medical Improvement." He reached inside his pants, adjusting his groin. "I guess people didn't really believe that Rod went through my head. He wanted to eliminate the doubters, shut up the skeptics."

Gene stood up, looked around like there was something he was looking for, and not finding it, resumed counting.

"A big man. Doc Bigelow. professor of surgery at Harvard. Do you know what he brought out right before me, this big man? What preceded me in his little show to set the stage?"

Gene went over to the desk and picked up a notepad and pen. Then he went back to the floor to start again.

"A remarkable stalagmite."

Phin leaned down and watched Gene closely. Then he uttered in a low voice, right above his head, "Remarkable for its singular resemblance to …" Phin leaned in and whispered into Gene's ear: "A petrified penis."

Gene scribbled out the tallies on the pad, ripped off the paper, crumpled it, and threw it toward the wastebasket. Phin dodged the crumpled paper, which sailed past his head and landed on the floor.

"That one I had no problem dodging," he winked. On the screen, the group walked down the corridor to meet the wizard.

"No wonder they thought of me as a freak. No wonder people say I was begging on the very steps of the building he presented me in," Phin snarled. He moved his head side to side as he sang, "The Massachusetts Medical College of Harvard University." Phin fell to his knees, right beside Gene. "We did beg, didn't we, Rod? Yes, we did … I think …" He searched the ceiling again. "Oh, damn this confusion. How I wish I could remember my own life!" He crawled on his knees closer to Gene, who was carefully stacking bills and writing tallies on the pad. "Please, sir, can you spare some change? Please. I have a hole in my head. I'll let you see it. Feel it. Spare a bit to feel a bit of brain?"

Gene carefully arranged the stacks of bills.

Phin looked over to the digital clock. It was 1:17 in the morning. For a moment it seemed like the minutes were sliding by erratically, the red electric numbers like something falling, bouncing, out of control. He rubbed his eyes and the clock was normal. It was 1:18.

"He's having trouble counting, Rod," Phin said. "Add it to the list." Phin stood up. He went over, picked up his skull cap, and regarded himself in the mirror. He put the cap back on and tied it, wiggling his jaw. The Scarecrow cowered in the wizard's presence.

"Doc Bigelow." He spat on the floor then picked up his tamping iron and rubbed the inscription with his finger. "He put the wrong date on you, Rod. Never mind misspelling my name. Twice. It's like a scar. You have yours and I have mine." He sneered at his reflection, fingering his scar. "The Big Harvard Man. Not much of a speller." He cradled the tamping iron, rocked it like a small child. "You've forgiven me, right, Rod? Well, I'll say it again. I'm so sorry I let him take you. But I wouldn't let him keep you. He did try. He wanted to separate us. But I didn't let him. I kept us together, Rod." He hugged the iron close, squeezed it to his chest, and sighed. "We'll always be together."

Gene was putting the money back in the bag.

Phin closed his eyes and breathed deeply. He opened his eyes and stared again at the clock. It seemed frozen, like time itself had stopped. Finally, another minute clicked by and he looked back to the TV. He scratched his head through the cap as Dorothy on mute scolded the wizard for being mean to the lion.

"A tamping iron," he said. "Now that's a tool. Perfect design for the job it's intended for. Are you ready for that, Gene? Because they're going to use you like a tool. Like an inkblot. Any quack or loony who has a theory about the brain will use your case as justification. You wait. They did it to me."

Gene walked past him, picked up his phone, and went into the bathroom.

"Once a journalist gets a hold of your story, then it's gone with the wind. It will grow and rise just like your so-called comedy performances. And now, with this thing you speak of, this inter-net: I can't even imagine. It will spread like your fires, in a matter of seconds—myth, gossip, legend."

Phin went back to watching the clock. Again the minutes seemed stuck, unable to move. He watched and finally went over and shook the clock. The numbers floated out into the air, dripping into streams of light. Then the streams formed letters, then words, then a sentence in cursive: No longer Gage. Phin screamed and dropped the clock.

"Brain Damage" came on.

"What the hell?" Gene shouted as he stormed out of the bathroom, his pants around his ankles. "What did you do that for?" he asked.

Phin held Rod tightly and looked at the upside-down clock.

"Lunatic," Gene said and picked up his phone on the desk. "I can't listen to this shit anymore," he said under his breath, more to himself. He took his phone with him back into the bathroom.

Springsteen's "I'm on Fire" came on.

Phin held the tip of the iron close to his face and, kicking the pieces of clock away, regained his composure. "Surprise," he said. "More fire songs!" He shook his head and turned toward the bathroom. "You'll be a blank sheet—even the writers and poets will use you. The mind. Personality. It's all just so *fascinating*."

Gene grunted as he defecated.

"Could you turn the fan on, please?" Phin said. "That's another thing we have in common—fetid odors. You like that one, Rod? Me too. I know what Gene will say though."

Phin looked from the TV to the mirror for his impersonation. "We're not the same." He turned away from his reflection with a sneer, sat down on the bed, picked up the remote, and started playing with the buttons. The monkeys were attacking the group in the forest. "Gene, these buttons, on this device—"

"Shut the fuck up!" Gene shouted. Phin held his breath as the monkeys flew away with Toto and Dorothy. When he saw the Scarecrow lying on the Haunted Forest floor, ripped apart, he screamed.

"What the fuck is it?" Gene came out of the bathroom, his pants still around his ankles.

Phin pointed as he reached for his flask.

"It's just TV," Gene said. "It's not real. For fuck's sake." He turned it off and went back to the bathroom. Phin took another drink.

"Ahh, that's better. Like hell we're not the same. Rod has checked all the boxes ten times over. That sounded like fitful, irreverent profanity to me. And where do you think I get this booze? I certainly can't buy it. What was the word you called me—a wraith? Yes, that's it. They don't sell alcohol to wraiths. Not even in California."

Gene shouted again.

"Coarse? Check. Vulgar? Check. Lacking restraint? Bull's-eye," Phin said. He counted on his fingers. "Capricious. Obstinate. Impatient. Trouble concentrating. I would say that covers it." He shrugged. "And we're not even talking about this whole irrational plan of yours. Madness, sheer and total madness."

Phin sat on the edge of the unmade bed and took another small sip. Gene flushed and washed his hands. Phin scratched his droopy eyelid.

"Here. It's lotion," Gene said, handing the small bottle over as he came out of the bathroom. "It helps with the itching."

Phin opened the container and smelled it. He squeezed a dab onto his palm, inspected it, and rubbed his hands together.

Gene lay down on the bed and closed his eyes.

"Hmmm, yes, even the writers and poets will use you, probably without even consulting medical reports," Phin said, squeezing more lotion and applying it to his legs. "Fabrication. Distortion. I can only imagine the kind of mush they'll come up with, some desperate novelist with too much ego and not enough imagination, thinking he's being so clever. Using you. Just to get published."

The Stones' "Play with Fire" started.

"I've always wanted to write poetry—if only I didn't have what they called the intellectual capacity of a child. How about a poem, Rod?"

Rod scratched the following words into the wall.

Holes in the world
Holes in your mind
Holes that hide things
Nobody will find.

"Lovely!" Phin exclaimed. "Another!"

Carts for golf
Carts pulled by an ox
Carts for the headless
When they're in a box

"Not bad, not bad," Phineas said, screwing the cap onto the lotion, then unscrewing his flask. "Another."

Matter that is gray
Matter that is white
Matter that doesn't matter
No not quite.

He downed the remaining liquid in the flask, shaking the final drops into his gaping mouth. "That's good for what ails you," he said, punctuating the sentence with a guttural belch. Then in one motion he ripped his skull cap off and tossed it. "Screw this infernal cap. Genie, can we turn the TV back on?"

Monday, December 4th, 2017

Nick barely slept that week in the hotel bed that felt empty with too many pillows. Ashley didn't return his calls or texts. None of the hospitals would tell him anything, and his in-laws wouldn't answer his texts or calls either. When he did sleep, he had a recurring dream of himself in his elementary school art class. It was all so vivid: the smell of paint and clay, the stools, the tables, Mrs. Doyle and her llama smock. Nick was drawing Chicago Bears players on an enormous canvas. In a flurry, his hand would draw lifelike renderings of the Bears' vaunted 46 defense: Steve McMichael, Dan Hampton, the Fridge William Perry, Iron Mike Singletary. The helmets and face masks were all perfect and accurate for each player. The drawings would come to life and line up across from a pulpit. Suddenly a drawing of his dad in a Packers uniform would appear, wearing a helmet with the single bar, like a kicker. But instead of the green G, his yellow helmet had a green cross. Nick could only watch as his father climbed up into the pulpit, young and healthy and serene, in a single ray of light. The ball would be snapped to his father, smacking him in the chest, before the Bears defense surged forth and pummeled him. Horror-struck and helpless, Nick watched the ball get snapped again and again as his dad would get more and more mangled and battered. But also the Bears players. Their very skulls and helmets would swell with each hit until they lumbered about on the page like giant deformed bobble heads. Finally, with one last gruesome hit, their heads would explode as his father emitted one last groan of anguish. From the bottom of the pile of bodies, the fire would start and he would hear his father's voice.

"Nick, have you practiced piano yet today?" Then he would awaken in a cold sweat.

*

Phineas turned from regarding Gene's sleeping face to glance at the hotel alarm clock, still lying upside down on the floor. It was 2:15 in the afternoon.

"Not the rescue," Gene muttered in his sleep. "I can reach them with an iron."

Phineas stood and opened the curtain. Sunlight streamed in, shining on Gene's face.

Gene roused, yawned, sat up, and stretched. He rubbed the sleep from his eyes and looked over at Phineas.

"Where did you get that?" Gene asked.

"From your old classroom," Phineas said, adjusting his bow tie in the mirror with one hand and holding a model skeleton with the other. He set the educational model skeleton down on the hotel desk and put on his jacket. The model was a yard long, held up by a small stand with a metal pole. "You know the one near your desk, that you put all your teaching badges on as a joke?" he said. He retied his bow tie in the mirror.

"That's not my property," Gene said. "It belongs to the school." He went into the bathroom and washed his face. He wiped his face with a towel and encountered a task he had left half-completed. He stood over the sink and resumed pouring gasoline from a red gas can into water bottles.

"*Now* we're concerned with property?" Phineas said, examining the base of the model's skull. "Properties of people. Properties of matter. Either way, perpetual change." He shrugged. "You know, in my case they never determined the place of entry nor exit with any precision. Doc Harlow saved my life, but he was a phrenologist."

"You have no right to take the school's educational materials," Gene said. He picked up his room key and suitcase, tucked the red gas can and the water bottles under his arm, and grabbed the black canvas bag with his free hand. With his elbow, he opened the door, used his foot to prop it open, and went out to the hall.

"So touchy," Phineas said, taking the tamping iron and the skeleton with him, making it out just as the door closed.

The water bottles were slipping. Gene walked quickly out of the hotel and across the parking lot. He made it to the car, set the items down on the ground, and started searching his pockets for his keys.

Phineas crouched to examine the gas can. "'NO SPILL,' it says. Designed like a human skull. Is that irony, Rod?"

Gene turned with livid eyes. He bent down into Phineas's face. "For. The. Love. Of. God. Shut up!"

Phineas watched Gene go back inside the hotel. He returned with his golf clubs and car keys in hand. He put the clubs, the can, and the black canvas bag in the back of the trunk. He closed it and went back inside, to the room. Phineas followed.

"Is the science teacher unfamiliar with phrenology? Or should I say pseudoscience teacher? I might have touched upon some more irony here, Rod. The pseudoscience teacher is unfamiliar with a pseudoscience."

Gene sat at the desk in the hotel room and checked the traffic on his phone.

"We'll be in the car," Phineas said, picking up his iron and the skeleton. "It's a problem of emotion. He can't feel his emotions properly," he said to the objects he was carrying as he walked out the door.

Gene did a once-over of the room, checking under the beds, behind the door, in the drawers.

Phineas leaned the tamping iron against the car, put the skeleton in the driver's side back seat, and buckled its seatbelt. "I'm glad you asked, Rod," he began, grabbing the iron and walking around the car. He opened the door of the back seat on the passenger's side. "Phrenology states that your personality can be inferred from the shape of your skull." He once again leaned the iron against the car, removed his jacket, folded it, and placed it on the middle seat. He studied his reflection. With a glance at the sky, he untied his bow tie and pulled the flask from his pocket. He took a two-gulp swig, put the tamping iron on top of the jacket, and got in next to his items. "Harlow believed I had damaged my organs of benevolence and veneration, the ones closest to heaven. Can you imagine? What nonsense. Pardon me, Rod." Phin reached over and petted the skull of the model, moving his hand from its forehead to the back of the skull. "Thus I became a slave to the grosser organs near the base of my skull, furthest away from heaven. Closest to you-know-who."

Gene got in the driver's seat and started the car.

"I wonder, Gene, do you think Harlow used standard units to measure the distance from my brain to heaven? What would the pseudoscientific standard unit of length be, an angel's wing?"

Gene turned on NPR. Two newscasters discussed the ramifications of Michael Flynn's guilty plea for lying to the FBI. Phin rolled down the rear passenger window.

"Not even a joke can lighten up old Genie," Phin said. "One of his moods. Did you know, Gene, what I was about to say, right before my accident?"

Gene pulled out of the parking lot and accelerated.

"I was going to say a joke to my coworker. 'Watch out Dooey! I had a lot of beans for lunch!' That's why I turned my head—to say my little joke to my coworker Dave Duerson, not realizing that the sand hadn't been poured. Just one spark from ol' Rod here striking rock. I opened my mouth, but the words never came out. I guess that's another similarity between us, Genie Boy. We both have jokes trapped on the thresholds of our minds, never to be uttered, stuck there for an eternity."

Gene hit a red light and turned off the radio. He switched the audio to his phone, which started playing Ben Harper's "Burn One Down," and merged onto Interstate 5, heading north. Phin rolled the windows up and down.

"One spark. Just like that. No longer Gage."

Gene weaved around the traffic of the right lanes to get into the left one, in time to catch the connection that would take him to Interstate 15. "Can you please leave the windows alone?" he asked over his shoulder in a tired voice.

"They exhumed my body," Phin said. "Pulled it right out of the ground in San Fran, to get my skull. My brother-in-law personally delivered it. Now that's family for you."

Gene hit the connector, changed lanes again, and rolled up Phin's window. Phin rolled it right back down. Gene got to the leftmost lane, accelerated, and jammed the rear window-up button. Phin responded, pressing and holding his window-down button. They each held on with the window frozen halfway. They rode east together in silence, the skeleton like a child in the rear seat, a strange family.

"Maybe you'll get exhumed too," Phin said finally. He released the button. "If they don't take out your brain when you die."

Gene rolled the window up and hit the child safety lock. He reached Interstate 15 and zoomed north. "I'll treat you like a child if I have to," he said.

"They moved my headless body," Phin said. He pulled the lid of the skull off the skeleton. "Why don't we forget about your act tonight, Gene? Call it off. We could go visit my old headless bones?"

The afternoon traffic slowed them down, but only a little.

"You know, Gene," Phin said. "They had a coffin ready for me, when the fungus was growing from my skull. They thought I was a goner. It was an infection. Cerebral abscess. Nothing a little silver nitrate couldn't take care of. That was two weeks after the blast. Once they got that taken care of, I was back on my feet, walking the piazza of Cavendish, Vermont. Beautiful town. We should all go there! Whaddya guys say? Road trip? I know Rod's on board."

Gene ignored him and drove, darting in and out of the congested lanes. Phin drank from his flask and fingered the opening in his skull. He pulled a small fragment of brain from the opening and examined it. He said in an ominous, sarcastic tone, "No longer Gene."

The traffic thickened to the point Gene could no longer weave through it. He cut his way across four lanes, swerved onto the shoulder, and accelerated to the off-ramp. In Escondido, he got confused, the navigation twice having him make a U-turn, until he finally arrived and drove right past the entrance to the Vineyards at Escondido. Gene followed a road around a bend before stopping on a street along the 6th hole. He shifted the car into park.

"Can you unlock the windows please?"

"No."

"Please. It's hot."

"No. Stop asking."

"Please."

"I said stop asking."

"But I'm *hawwwwt*. Rod here is practically burning up."

Gene watched the golf course.

"My brain is melting, melting," Phin said in a shrill voice, imitating the witch he had seen earlier. He winked at Rod, laughed, and took another drink.

Gene tapped the steering wheel with his fingers.

"You know, the early dissectionists generally did not fix or harden the brain before dissection. It limited what they could demonstrate. Also, they only sectioned it transversely—or you could say across, horizontally—for centuries. It wasn't until 1641 that Sylvius had his fissure drawings published. Gene, are you listening? Isn't this fascinating?"

Gene grunted.

"Rod used your phone while you were sleeping. I told him not to, but he wanted to show me how the inter-net is on your phone. I did some research. Wick-ed-pee-dee-um or something. After all, I did graduate from that 'unfit' one-room schoolhouse they called a school, or at least I think I did? Ah, blast it, what does it matter? Blast it … a pun. Look out, Rod, I'm going to steal the show from Gene."

Gene glanced at him in the rearview mirror, then out the window to the golf course.

"In the 1800s, they finally used a mixture of alcohol and an alkali on brain tissue," Phin said, sipping his flask and picking at his scalp. "By the 1840s they figured out how to freeze sections on slides for microscopes. Stains came around in 1858, right around the time Yours Truly went to San Francisco. Near the end. Localization studies on the brain—Gene? Are you listening?"

Gene stared out the window.

"That's all there is to it, Rod," Phin said, flicking a small piece of brain out the window. "He's not listening to us. Words won't help us. It's action we need. We've got to find a way to release the pressure on his brain."

*

"The policy is in her name, so I can't divulge any information, sir."

"Yes, you've said that," Nick said then swallowed two Advil.

"Sir, why don't you have your wife call back when she is available?"

"I don't know when that will be."

"Sir, the only way I can divulge—"

"Can you transfer me to your manager? I'm sick of hearing you say 'divulge.'"

Nick sat on hold, his head pounding. He scanned an article on the likelihood of the Bears firing John Fox. He preferred that to thinking about how to explain the current status of his marriage to the next representative of his insurance company.

"Hello?"

"Yes, this is Nick Moy. I'm inquiring about two fifteen-dollar copays for my wife's prenatal visits last week. They should be covered under our health plan."

"Yes, well, I'd be happy to help you look into this matter. Sometimes the doctors put in a code that creates a different charge, usually for special tests or for various circumstances."

"Yes. Well, since I'm being charged thirty dollars, I'd like to know what these special tests are."

"Sir, unfortunately I can't divulge …"

After yelling an obscenity at the top of his voice, Nick slammed his phone five times in quick succession against his desk. When he received the text about two water bottles filled with gasoline being found in a hotel parking lot in Pacific Beach, he looked at it through a web of cracked glass.

*

A twosome drove off. Gene scanned the course with his binoculars. He got out of the car, pulled his clubs from the trunk, jumped over the fence with his golf bag, and wasted no time setting up. He teed the ball up and sprinkled the powder. "Where the hell did I put those water bottles?" Gene went back to the car and searched the back seat and the trunk. Then he searched again.

"This golf, it appears to be a game of routines," Phin said, yawning in the back seat. "That's what Gene needs. Look at him. He's all out of sorts because his normal routine has been disrupted."

Gene cursed and slammed the trunk, causing Phin to jump. With heavy eyelids, he watched Gene hurdle the fence and walk toward the 6th tee. "Time for a rest," he said. "My, how a body gets tired."

Gene looked out from just off the tee and, again, he saw the bored faces, the disgruntled and unhappy and sad growing-older faces of people worn down by a lifetime of disappointments. He took a practice swing and stepped out on the stage.

Except that now the faces confused him. They were not the faces of an audience in a comedy club, eager for laughter, but the faces of students in his science class. And instead of teaching a lesson on the Crosscutting Concept of Cause and Effect to second graders, he was making a comparison between male and female sex drives and Mexican food. Instead of smiles, the children's faces showed confusion, perplexity, even a hint of disgust.

He turned to the other side of the fairway and, squinting in the imaginary spotlight, thought he saw a group of third graders. He asked them how they would design an experiment on forces using magnets and paperclips.

The spotlight, since it was actually the sun, was blinding. So he held up his hand to shield his eyes, only to discover that *this* side was a sold-out comedy club and he was doing a third grade science lesson, much to the growing dissatisfaction of the audience. He whirled around and then couldn't tell which side was which until, overwhelmed and crying out in frustration, he fled the scene.

*

Nick drove along listening to Monday Night Football on his radio. He pulled into the drive-thru line at the In-N-Out Burger near his hotel. The line curled around the block. He didn't care about the wait. He just wanted to grab a burger, get back to the hotel, watch the end of the game, eat, and fall asleep. He was tired. He was numb. He turned off the radio and let his mind drift.

Nick graduated college in 2000, the same year the Bears drafted Brian Urlacher. He landed a job in the Chicago suburbs selling diamond saw blades with a couple of his childhood friends. The job was thrown to him like a floatation device from one of his friends at Illinois State. Recognizing the opportunity to not pay rent and save money, he moved home. He had health insurance and bought a car. Nick didn't go to church. He watched the Bears religiously every Sunday with Gene, Dave, and Jimmy. They called it Bear Down. It was 2001. They usually watched the games in Dave's basement. Except one Sunday in October, they scored tickets and went to Soldier Field to watch the Bears defeat the Arizona Cardinals 20–13. After the game at the Big City Tap, Nick met Haley, a kindergarten teacher in the suburbs, also living at home, who would become his first serious girlfriend.

That season the Bears had five come-from-behind wins and won the NFC Central. His headaches were infrequent. Haley joined her first Bear Down for the Divisional Playoffs, a home matchup versus the Eagles. And even though the favored Bears got throttled 33–19, overall, life was good.

The leadership of the Riverside Asian Christian Church, operating remotely, finally made a switch and sent a new pastor. Nick's father was given an early service, from seven until ten in the morning, when he would rail about the eternal fires of Hell to the remaining five faithful—the last grizzled die hards that would not leave him. Half of his flock had disabilities, so it was the disabled preaching to his own. Despite the church undergoing a remodeling and temporarily holding services at a local middle school, attendance at the ten thirty service rebounded.

In 2002, Soldier Field also underwent remodeling. The Bears played their home games downstate, at Memorial Stadium on the campus of the University of Illinois in Champaign. Bear Downs resumed in Dave's basement. The season started out promising, with the Bears 2–0, but, like life in the suburbs when you're in your early twenties, things started to fall apart. The Bears went on an eight-game losing streak. Nick's father, growing more confused and nonsensical, harassed him daily about practicing the piano and his grades, threatening to take away his car keys.

After the season, enough was enough. The Bears drafted Rex Grossman and opened the renovated Soldier Field. Nick, Gene, Dave, and Jimmy got an apartment in Wrigleyville. Things were looking up. Gene and Dave did improv at the Last Laugh. Jimmy started a PhD program in neuropsychology at DePaul University, and Nick got promoted to manager.

It was a good year. The city was full of life. But, as the Bears muddled along to a 7–9 record, for Nick something seemed off. His headaches returned. Haley shared her concerns one evening when Nick seemed listless and remote. He couldn't put his finger on it, but it was like there was something out there that he desperately needed, some feeling or want, and he knew he would never attain it.

In January 2004, the Bears hired Lovie Smith, and Nick's company offered him a transfer to San Diego. Nick brought Haley along for a visit. They took off during a freezing rainstorm and landed in seventy-degree sunshine. Nick didn't have a single headache on the trip, and Lovie Smith promised to beat the Packers and win a Super Bowl. On the flight home, Haley and Nick decided to move to San Diego together. They were engaged over the summer. An elementary school in El Cajon, just east of San Diego, hired Haley after a phone interview.

The first year in San Diego was challenging. They didn't know anyone. Starting in September, Haley came dutifully with Nick to watch Bears games at a bar in Pacific Beach. But it was strange, watching games at ten a.m. and sitting in a bar for four hours instead of being outside in the warm sun. Rex Grossman got hurt. The Bears went 5–11. Haley was homesick. Her kindergarten class was a nightmare. Planning the wedding was stressing her out. It seemed like every time she needed help, Nick was having headaches.

Somehow, the wedding got planned. They moved to a different apartment, and Nick got a satellite TV so he could watch the Bears games on the couch. Also, his neighbor Harris was a Bears fan so he would come over, which took the pressure off Haley to sit around on Sunday. On the strength of their defense, their running game, and rookie Kyle Orton's mistake-free game management, the Bears cruised to an 11–5 record.

They were married in January, surrounded by friends and family, on the beach in La Jolla, same weekend as the NFC Divisional Playoff game versus the Carolina Panthers. Despite the upset win for Carolina, at the same time that Panthers receiver Steve Smith told postgame reporters, "If you lined up my mama out there, I got to catch it over her, too," Haley told Nick everything was going to be OK. And he believed her.

And during their first year as a married couple in 2006, things indeed were very good. One evening in October, Nick and Harris discovered Rosie's bar as a prime spot to watch Monday Night Football. The same night that the Bears came from behind to beat the Cardinals and Arizona head coach Dennis Green told postgame reporters, "You wanna crown them, crown their ass!" Nick's boss called to tell him he had made assistant manager. His headaches were nonexistent. The Bears made it to the Super Bowl. Devin Hester returned the opening kickoff for a tuddy. Haley whispered to Nick that she wanted to start a family. And even though the Bears eventually lost to the Colts in a driving rainstorm, Nick agreed. They started trying that night.

Behind him in the In-N-Out line, a car honked. Nick crept up the two empty car lengths in front of him. He turned the game back on, but there was an injury time-out, so he turned it back off and stared out at the palm trees waving in the breeze.

*

Rosie O'Grady's Pub
Monday Night Football Week 13
Pittsburgh Steelers vs. Cincinnati Bengals

On Cincinnati's first possession of the game, Steelers linebacker Ryan Shazier tackled Bengals wide receiver Josh Malone. It looked like a normal everyday tackle until Shazier didn't get up. He lay on the field, clutching his back. Three large screens showed the replay.

"That could be a spinal cord issue," Jimmy said.

"It didn't look serious," Mike said.

"Look at his legs. They're not moving at all. Bad sign. Not good."

Harris, Mike, and Jimmy had forsaken the usual seats and sat in the three center stools. They had Steelers fans on the right side, Bengals fans on the left. They ordered more beers and a basket of nachos.

Dave texted from Phoenix: *Someone fart on my seat for me. Don't shart though.*

Mike replied: *Too late*

Harris added a winking poo emoji.

The training staff was putting Shazier on a stretcher.

"You guys talk to Nick this week?" Mike asked.

"Not since I found out about his house," Jimmy said, pulling out a cheesy chip. "Sucks. How's he doing? Does he need a place to stay?"

A cart drove out onto the field. All the players were standing around. Some were praying. The cameras focused on a somber Big Ben.

"It's not just his house," Harris said, chewing and wiping his fingers. "He came by to watch the Bears yesterday."

"Don't tell me," Mike said with a straight face. "He watched the Bears?"

Harris smiled. "No. It's quite serious. You know how they've been having that issue with the golf balls. His wife Ashley was hit last Monday. The morning of the fire. In the stomach."

"Shit."

"And she's pregnant."

"I didn't know she was pregnant."

"They didn't tell anyone," Harris said. "It was pretty recent."

Dave texted: *Just ask Betsy for a moist towelette. She'll know what to do.*

"First Gene and now Ashley," Mike said. "What is it with these San Diego golfers?"

"Is the baby OK?" Jimmy asked.

"Nick doesn't know. I guess they've been having some issues and aren't talking. Nick's all torn up."

Mike replied again: *The Moist Towelettes. That's a good name for our a cappella group.*

"Sucks," Jimmy said.

Dave texted back: *I'm game, as long as we cover Africa.*

They drove Shazier out through the tunnel.

Monday Night Football results Week 13
Pittsburgh Steelers 23 Cincinnati Bengals 20

*

Nick watched the leaves of the palm trees swaying, thinking back to the year 2006, hearing Haley's voice telling him everything was going to be OK …

The next year the Great Recession hit, the Bears stumbled their way to last place in their division, and a rift developed between Haley and Nick. She wanted to move home. His headaches came back, stronger than ever.

"Brutal," Nick texted his friends, referring to both the Bears' anemic offense and the frozen construction industry—the buyers of the blades he was selling.

Financially, the first bad year wasn't too bad because they had a little money saved up. But the second year was indeed pretty bad. Haley still had temporary teacher status, and her school let her go. She began substitute teaching, and even that wasn't consistent. So when the third year went from bad to worse, Nick was looking for a way out of the construction industry. Haley and Nick fought constantly over three main subjects: money, moving back to Chicago, and the results from the clinic showing his infertility. She wanted to take out a loan for treatment.

"I'm not paying for it, and that's final," he said.

The Bears missed the playoffs all three years.

In April of 2009, the Bears traded for Jay Cutler and Nick met Doug Jordan. They were bench-pressing next to each other at the gym when they each needed a spot.

"Let me give you a hand there," Doug said, coming to Nick's aid.

They were both from Chicago. Doug was wearing a Cutler #6 T-shirt.

"I grew up in Riverview," Nick said, sliding another five pounds onto each side.

"No kidding," Doug said, sipping a protein shake. "I grew up in Vernonshire."

"Are you as excited as I am about Cutty?"

Nick told him about slinging blades. Doug shared how he worked in private security and made decent money installing and maintaining security systems.

"No one feels safe," Doug said as Nick strained under the bar. "Recessions will come and go, but crime is like sex: It's always going to be around."

They finished the workout together.

"Shoot me a text if you want to hang out sometime," Doug said when they were done. "Maybe catch a game."

The economy stumbled out of the Great Recession. Nick wasn't lying when he told his mom over the phone, "Things are OK now."

"And your headaches? Are you taking your medication?"

"Yeah, mom. I am. Don't worry. They're not too bad right now."

His job rebounded. As if ordained by the cosmos, Gene and Dave moved to San Diego. His marriage with Haley hardened into something resembling stability. He agreed to trying some of the low-end treatments for infertility.

They resurrected Bear Down. Nick hosted. His neighbor Harris, along with Doug and Gene, came faithfully every Sunday. Dave started traveling for stand-up, but managed to make appearances as the Bears reached the NFC Championship. For Nick, life felt full again, his headaches were more or less under control, and things did seem like they were going to work out after all.

But it was a tease, like the treatments at the infertility clinic. Lovie Smith's Bears fell short once again. To Aaron Rodgers and the Packers.

Another honk from behind, but by this time Nick had progressed through the In-N-Out line and was sitting at a red light. He drove toward the hotel, munching on his fries, his head pounding. He parked and started walking to his room, until he realized his hotel card was in his wallet, which was in his car. He walked back toward the car, sipping his milkshake, his mind stuck on the reruns of his life.

In 2012, the Bears acquired Brandon Marshall and appeared to be one of the league's elite teams, opening with a 7–1 record. Nick and Doug's friendship had matured, much like their gradually increasing combined bench-press max. Three pastimes emerged as staples in their relationship: lifting weights, NFL football, and going to strip clubs. When Haley found out about the third pastime, she left Nick and moved back to Chicago, though the divorce would not be final for another few years.

The Bears roster turned out to be fool's gold. They stumbled to an 8–8 record as Nick and Doug abandoned Bear Down and went off on their own. Sometimes, from the haze of a nightclub with a stripper on his lap, during a commercial for an NFL game, or resting between sets at the gym, he would hear his father's voice, strained but booming from the wheelchair next to the pulpit. It was like Mozart or Beethoven or Chopin. It just popped to the surface from deep in his brain.

"THERE IS NO HEAT LIKE THE FIRE OF HELL! REPENT! BEFORE YOU BURN FOR AN ETERNITY IN THE DAMNING FLAMES AND BRIMSTONE OF GOD'S WRATH!"

*

Gene was driving south aimlessly. He glanced in his rearview mirror. Phin lay passed out with the tamping iron in his arms. The skeleton leaned on him like a small child sleeping.

The fire had not started. He had flopped. It was not a good performance. Something was off. He didn't trust his instincts. His mind played a trick on him, telling him that he wasn't a world-famous comedian, merely a science teacher at an elementary school. But it was just a trick. He knew who he was.

"You know," Phin slurred from the back seat with both eyes closed. "I did make a couple of public appearances. I can remember one at Barnum's American Museum in New York City—which isn't related to Barnum's circus. Just a few here and there, mostly around New England, because the opportunity was there. And they paid. So why wouldn't I?" He turned, muttering. "And now I'm remembered as this sideshow freak … traveling the country … begging and drinking … erroneous stories, works of fiction that people actually read."

You can't always be on the top of your game, Gene thought. It was an off night. He had been feeling tired. All the top comedians had a flop once in a while. But he knew who he was. And he would rise again, higher than ever before.

"Memory," Phin said, before turning back to the window. "It's bound to slip."

*

Nick tossed the burger wrapper away, took his medication, and turned out the lights, but he couldn't sleep. His mind wouldn't let him, like a teacher demanding he pay attention. He sat and listened to his own inexorable past, starting again on New Year's Eve 2012. Nick was hungover, but Doug had managed to drag him to the gym. The Bears had just fired Lovie Smith.

Doug punched Nick in the shoulder.

"Check it out," he said, sipping his protein shake. "I got a text from a buddy last night. Dude works as an arson investigator. Like a PI. A detective, a dick, except for fire. A fire dick."

"You do love dick," Nick said.

"Haha, very funny," Doug said. "Listen, this could be our ticket. He says there's a lot of money in becoming an arson detective. He gets contracted at the local, state, and even federal level. Wildfires are getting crazier and crazier."

"Yeah?" Nick said. He winced as the vise of his headache tightened.

"Benefits, paid leave, vacation days, and a pension," Doug said, waving his protein shake like a good job and an easy life was just a sip away. "Think it over."

"I don't know," Nick said. Then, to change the subject: "Who are the Bears going to hire?"

"Who knows?" Doug said.

The next time they went to the gym, Doug showed up with a brochure for the two-year program to become a Certified Fire Investigator. Later that day, Nick's saw blade boss called him with the news that there would be a slight pay cut for the next six months. It was all the incentive Nick needed. He didn't even give two weeks' notice. Next Sunday the Bears hired Marc Trestman, and Nick called home to borrow some money from his parents to help pay for college and his divorce.

Tuesday, December 5th, 2017

This time Gene didn't listen to music. He didn't have a desk in a hotel. He didn't have a phone or a bag of cash. What he had was a golf bag with fourteen clubs, some kind of makeshift workshop behind a blanket hanging from a branch under a sagging tree leaning beneath the Eight overpass, and a curious, newly acquired reputation amongst San Diego's homeless population. He was Jeeves, the Homeless Golfer. The crowd would laugh and hurl insults. A toothless man had tagged him with the nickname and it had stuck among a small group that huddled nearby. They were like an unruly gallery in some dystopian golf novel. Gene would pace the pavement, head down, carrying his clubs like he was debating a strategy on a faraway fairway at a critical stage of some tournament in his mind.

"How many shots under par are you today, Jeeves?"

"Can't find your ball, Jeeves?"

"You're not keeping your elbow in, Jeeves!"

"Dammit, Jeeves! Can't you get some of them birdies?"

The gallery sat like a murder of crows, waiting to caw. Gene emerged from his makeshift workshop with his bag of clubs. And a strange grin on his face. And a box of matches. He walked along, carrying his clubs, ignoring the gallery and the omnipresent sound of a horse following behind him.

"Keep your head down, Jeeves!"

*

Nick woke up and drove to Escondido. A well-informed golfer had found tees coated with match heads matching a description of those used by the Links Lighter. He pulled onto the 163 going north, and the reruns in his head started again.

In 2012, Marc Trestman's first year, Nick and Doug began the Certified Fire Investigator program at Southwestern College in Otay Mesa. They visited over fifty fire sites that year. Nick was getting better, but he made a lot of mistakes too, like the 2013 Bears who went 8–8 for the season. Then, like Marc Trestman, he got another year under his belt, though unlike the 5–11 Bears, he actually seemed to be learning.

That December, the Bears fired Trestman and General Manager Phil Emory and hired Ryan Pace, who then went on to hire John Fox. And the Ed Bavera Fire Investigation Company hired both Nick and Doug as interns.

The Bears finished 6–10 that year, and, like Bears fans, Nick was growing impatient with his job. He was working as an intern for minimum wage with sporadic hours, mostly looking at individual home fires. Doug and Nick still worked out together three times a week and watched football on Sunday with Harris. Jimmy arrived in San Diego, a doctoral candidate in neuroscience at UCSD, and occasionally Gene (despite the birth of his second daughter) and Dave (despite his schedule on the road) made it for a Bear Down.

In 2016, Nick and Doug still enjoyed a monthly strip club binge. On a couch at Cheetah's, Doug convinced Nick to sign up for a twelve-week Criminal Investigators Training Program followed by a fifteen-week Special Agent Basic Training. The idea was that if they couldn't get work in fire investigation, a good backup plan would be to work with the Bureau of Alcohol, Tobacco, Firearms, and Explosives, better known as the ATF. Nick called home to get another loan.

"Sure, as long as you keep taking your medicine and come home to visit," his mom said. "And talk to Jimmy, I hear he's a brain doctor now!"

That January, as the NFL Wildcard weekend kicked off with the Bears once again missing the playoffs for the 2016 season, Nick decided to skip football and went to the gym by himself. He didn't feel up to bench-pressing. He decided to do a workout focusing entirely on his lower body. As he was doing a squat, he heard something he had never heard from his subconscious, deep in his brain alongside Mozart and his dad's admonition about the fires of Hell: his mom's voice.

He went home and started a profile on Match.com. A month later, after his third first date, he met Ashley.

They felt the chemistry from the first date. She was just like his mom: smart and practical and serious, but also goofy and kind. She worked in healthcare as a medical assistant and planned to become a nurse. In two weeks it was official; she was his girlfriend. In six months, she moved into his University Heights apartment.

Monday, December 11th, 2017

Comedy is a combination of timing and material, Gene thought from the shade. The material needs to be funny, true, and something people can relate to. The more common and relatable, the better. But even if you have good material, it's the timing that counts. Jokes are like golf swings. Most comedians waste their jokes by losing the energy too early. The golf swing is about harnessing energy—trapping it—until it explodes downward, through the club and into the golf ball. The same thing with jokes. You have to build up the energy, set up the laugh, and then *come down* with tremendous precision and timing.

He looked up and saw the helicopter. From under his tree he watched it go by, flying low.

"Easy girl, easy now … that's it," Phineas said, pulling the bridle. He was wearing a brightly colored poncho made of sheep's wool, a *chumpiru* (felt hat), and *ekota* (sandals). The horse was shiny and black.

The sound of the helicopter dwindled in the distance. It wasn't the material, Gene thought. It was my tempo. I had no tempo. The audience likes to be surprised, but not if they're too off-balance. You've got to stabilize them first. Get them grounded and comfortable. Draw them in. Then you can surprise the hell out of them, but first things first.

"Didn't you have animals in your science classroom? Guinea pigs and geckos and things? Taking care of animals is an excellent activity for brain injury. Adding structure to tasks, that's a key method for coping," chattered Phineas.

Smooth and steady. Let the jokes do the work. Don't force it or try too hard. People can sense desperation. Calm, with confidence. Smile a lot. Trust your game. Visualize them laughing, then make it happen. Execute. You're ready. The big time. You've paid your dues. It's time to set the world on fire.

They heard sirens in the distance. The horse neighed.

"There, there," Phineas said. "It's all right, baby." He pulled a carrot from under his poncho and fed the horse, stroking its neck.

*

It was ten o'clock on Monday morning. Nick was still trying to shake off the cobwebs from Sunday. For the second straight week he had gone to Harris's to watch the Bears. For the second straight week the Bears had lost and Nick and Harris got trashed. He took two Advil and was pouring his third cup of coffee when his phone buzzed. A chopper had sighted a lone golfer lingering around the Chula Vista Golf Course.

Nick arrived an hour later to the perimeter. Three police cars, a van with two FBI agents, and two fire trucks were assembled, discussing strategy. The idea was to surround the area around the golf course and slowly close in on the lone golfer like an animal. The focal point would be the 6th hole. Nick was given his position and a walkie-talkie. The temperature was over eighty degrees, unseasonably warm, with no wind. The golf course was brown with small patches of green for the putting surfaces. Even the fairways were dead. Nick was sweating profusely as he walked along a side road, alert for the Links Lighter lurking in the bushes. A rigid headache settled over his brain like someone forcing him to wear a hat three sizes too small.

There was not a shred of cloud in the sky. It was approaching noon. Nothing moved. Small diameters of shadow circled the trees, providing minimal shade. The air shimmered with heat. Nick regarded the hills and houses. It was like a pulse, he thought. Things were pulsing with heat. He wiped the sweat off his brow with the sleeve of his dark blue shirt, now soaked with perspiration. It drains you, this kind of heat. A pulsing stillness zaps you and drains you.

Nick received a text informing him of his position with a GPS marker and chose a spot in the shade of a palm tree. He glanced around, trying to seem inconspicuous. He watched from between two houses along the course as a foursome of old white men pulled up in the fairway. He looked at their shoes and their clothes and their hats. He watched the serious and methodical way one of them stood over a ball, staring down for nearly a minute before he finally hit it, the other three also serious and still. The one hitting must have been in his sixties, maybe pushing seventy. He wore a back brace over his bright orange golfing shirt. He also had a knee brace and a strap across his forearm.

"You're going to like it, Steve!" one of them shouted.

"Nice ball."

"Fucking absurd," Nick said to himself as the two carts slowly pulled away. "I can live the rest of my life without seeing another stupid golf course." The vise inside his head tightened. Everything shimmered.

*

The blistering heat of the day had faded. A light breeze had picked up from the west, bringing tantalizingly cool whiffs of air from the ocean. The shadows had grown as if to reward everything that had endured the heat of midday. Gene pulled out his binoculars. The coast was clear. Just Phineas and that damn horse.

He stepped out onto the 6th tee to a standing ovation. The audience loved him. They wanted to make it clear that they appreciated him. There were no lingering feelings from his recent egg of a performance. They knew what he was capable of. If anything, they loved him more because now he seemed more human, more flawed, more vulnerable, but also more tenacious and devoted to his craft of bringing the light of laughter into a dark world.

He stood out on the tee and soaked in the applause. Never had he felt so mortal and so alive at the same time. This was living. He shook his head from side to side, then a little jiggle for his shoulders, his wrists, his hips, his knees. He stretched his fingers like a pianist. The laughter was already going. He keenly felt his body and mind and imagination revving itself up. They loved him and needed him. It was time to deliver. To give the people what they wanted. Needed.

He played up the finger-stretching thing. The audience roared. They could tell that he was in fine form and they were in for the performance of a lifetime. A performance they would always remember. Life affirming. One to rally the soul, awaken lost dreams, ignite passions. It was time.

*

Nick moved stealthily into the next GPS position texted to him. He remained vigilant and saw an old woman looking at him strangely from her window about twenty feet away. He held up his badge so as to assuage any alarm she might feel at seeing a middle-aged Asian man in dark clothes slipping furtively through her neighbor's backyard. She still regarded him with curiosity, right on the edge of alarm.

He scrambled out from the yard to a position behind a comfort station on the golf course, in between the 12th and 13th holes. As he approached, the man with the braces on various body parts came out of the restroom. The man didn't see Nick and walked over to the 13th tee, where his group was teeing off. Nick crouched in the shade and watched them hit. Again, the brace guy took forever.

"Dammit!" another of them shouted after his drive. "Why do I keep going right?"

"That's a red stake, Otis," another said. "You can drop from up there."

They were gone. Nick was left with his thoughts, which resembled something whirring and clicking, vainly trying over and over again to latch on.

It was approaching five o'clock. As Nick did every weekday at five o'clock, he texted Ashley, knowing she was getting off work.

I love you.

*

Ed Cruz played in the Chula Vista Men's League every Monday morning. A retired custodian, he hadn't started playing golf until his late fifties. He played a few times with his new son-in-law in Arizona and got the bug. Once he retired at sixty-five, he started playing regularly and associated improving his golf game with improving his mind, staying fit, and honoring his commitments. He enjoyed the camaraderie and social aspects of the men's league. Plus, his wife liked having him out of the house.

With the steady play of retired life, he had managed to lower his handicap to an 18. Then this fall, he began breaking 90 with regularity. He was driving the ball farther than ever. He had his first eagle, holing out on a par 4. Before last week's round, he had been ranked 28th out of sixty-five men in the individual scoring, and his team was in second place. Then there was last week.

On the 12th hole, a par 5, he had 100 yards left. Out of nowhere, he hit a banana slice off the hosel of his wedge. He hit three more banana slices before picking up and taking an 8. On the last six holes, three times he had 100 yards to the pin and all three times he hit a banana slice off the hosel. It was mysterious, watching the ball curve wildly off to the right.

"Looks like you've been snake bit," Gerardo, his partner and a 9 handicap, said.

A key factor in his development was his ability to connect errors in his swing to the ball's trajectory. For example, if the club face was open, the ball sliced. When he swung inside out, a hook. But he had zero idea what could be causing the banana slice. He had been having a good round, a little below his average score, when the anomalous shot reared its ugly head. He blew up for a 107. It was his worst round in five years. He dropped to 46th and his team dropped to fourth.

He went to the range twice after that Monday and had no problems at all with his 100-yard wedge shot. As mysteriously as it had appeared, so too had it gone.

"I think I've figured it out," he said to Gerardo before they teed off for their next Monday match.

He had a fantastic start. On the first five holes he drained a 30-foot birdie, had two standard pars and a sandy par. With his one bogey, he was even par on the 6th tee, something he had never been before so deep into a round.

And then on the 6th fairway, 100 yards out, the banana slice reemerged. Again, the shot stumped him. He asked Gerardo to look at his swing. He checked his tempo, his takeaway, the position of his hands—all of it checked out.

"It's like the Boogeyman," Gerardo said.

The banana slice became a devil tormenting his round. He fired seven slices on the next three holes, including three shots in a row that went out of bounds.

By the time he came to the 10th tee, he had zero interest in playing the next nine holes and even considered quitting the game. Why spend so much money and time just to get myself so worked up? he thought. He was a shell of the golfer that had been ranked 28th. When he teed off, he barely hit the ball. He dinked the ball along two more holes until number 12, where he sliced one banana wedge more than his psyche could endure. The little splash of water seemed to mock him over the edge, and he fired his wedge into the water. He grabbed three more clubs and twirled them into nearby brush, screaming obscenities to the startled bunnies that ran for cover. His partners finally managed to restrain him, at which point he stomped off the course and went straight home, calming down just as he entered his house at eight thirty that morning.

"I'm quitting golf forever," he announced to his wife.

He took two Advil and lay down for a nap. When he awoke at ten a.m., the whole thing seemed like a ridiculous dream with everything blown out of proportion. His partners had brought his bag back and left it on the side of his garage. There were only twelve clubs, meaning two were still out there. He opened a beer and realized he had to figure out what was causing that banana slice. That he couldn't end his golfing life like that. He couldn't let it get the best of him.

Ed walked back to the course and crawled through the brush, finding his seven iron and then wading into the water barefoot to get his wedge. The course was nearly empty at midday. A foursome of two couples came through. He turned to walk back toward the clubhouse. He hit a bucket of balls on the range and struck every wedge crisply. It was all in his head. He would have to play to defeat whatever was playing tricks on his mind.

He started to walk home, but when he saw the 6th hole open from the road he decided to jump over the fence, slip through some houses, and drop a few balls from the 100-yard marker, returning, in his words (which would come off as ironic later in his statement), to the scene of the crime. Ed dropped a handful of balls and began hitting. He didn't really pay attention to the sound of the helicopter until it was close, almost right over him, flying low.

"Put your hands in the air," a voice boomed down from the helicopter.

He knew he wasn't supposed to walk out on the course like this, but what was going on? It was then that he saw two police officers dart out from behind a bush and charge him. The next thing he knew he had been tackled and had the wind knocked out of him. They stuck a knee in his back and handcuffed him. So he didn't have much air in his lungs as he gasped something about trying to fix his banana slice.

*

About seven miles away, on the 6th hole of the Salt Creek Golf Club, Gene could hear the sirens off in the distance as he swung repeatedly, as hard as he could. But the grass on the tee had recently been watered. In his heart he knew this, but his brain refused to accept it. He swung again and again, muttering tersely, resetting his doctored match head tees, breaking them occasionally, until he broke the last of the half dozen he had in his golf bag. He could not create the spark.

In his mind, the audience that had greeted him so enthusiastically stood patiently as he delivered his best material, big swing after big swing, until slowly they started heading for the exits, looking back with faces of disappointment.

He turned and watched as Phineas mounted his horse and rode off.

He had failed his audience. Again. When they needed him most. It was time to go.

*

Rosie O'Grady's Pub
Monday Night Football Week 14
New England Patriots vs. Miami Dolphins

Harris and Jimmy sat at a table on the patio. They could hear the pregame but couldn't see it. Patriots fans filled the bar like an infection.

"Dave's not getting back from Seattle until late," Harris said. "Mike said he was going to yoga but that he'd be back next week."

"It's just the two of us, I guess," Jimmy said.

"Just the two of us," Harris said. They clinked the necks of their bottles and drank. A different bartender came up, a guy they had never seen before.

"Where do all these Patriots fans get off?" Jimmy asked the new bartender. "Don't they know this is a Bears bar?"

"Huh?" the bartender said. He was young and very busy. Sweat ran down his face.

"Never mind," Harris said. "We'll take some fried mushrooms when you get a chance."

The game kicked off.

"Any update on Nick and Ashley?" Jimmy inquired. "Are they talking? Is the baby OK?"

"I only spoke with him briefly," Harris said. "He sounded really low."

"Poor guy. I can't imagine what he's going through."

"I'm worried about him," Harris said. "He told me he's thinking of giving up the NFL cold turkey. That it was pointless. A waste of time." The beer-battered mushrooms arrived. Harris picked one up and put it down quickly. "Hot," he said.

"I can see where he's coming from," Jimmy said. "But think, would we know each other if it wasn't for the Bears?"

"Probably not."

Jimmy picked up a mushroom with a fork. The steam poured out. He blew on it before eating it.

"Nick was telling me he thought there was something wrong with his brain," Harris said. "Like it wasn't functioning properly. *Damaged.* That's how he said it. He said he thought his brain had been damaged as a kid, in a car accident."

"Yeah, he cracked the windshield with his head," Jimmy said. "Not good."

Harris nodded. They ate the mushrooms and watched the game.

"Now I'm no golfer, but what are the odds?" Harris asked. "First Gene and now Nick's pregnant wife."

"They're not as rare as you might think," Jimmy said.

"You're a real statistician, aren't you?"

Jimmy laughed. "Naw, I'm a contrarian. A regular Walter Sobchak. Get yourself a nice robe and you can be the Dude. Did I ever tell you about the hat incident?"

"What happened again?" Harris asked, stuffing his face.

"Remember? Ocon's name was pulled first for both the fantasy draft order and the divisions. Basically, one out of twelve names. Then, the odds that his name, one of twelve, would be chosen again. Nick made me calculate the odds, which are less than one in a thousand. But those are actually good odds."

"Oh, right. I had forgotten all about it. But I remember the argument."

They laughed and finished the mushrooms. The Dolphins hit another field goal. At the table behind them a fan cheered. "All right baby, let's go!"

In the second quarter, burritos arrived and Cutler threw a touchdown to Jarvis Landry.

"What is it about Cutler?" Harris asked.

"It's his body language," Jimmy said. "He has no affect. People need to see emotion."

Then it was halftime.

"You know I played golf in high school, at Riverview Municipal Golf Course back in Illinois," Jimmy said as the new bartender cleared the plates. "I played quite a bit, growing up."

"I tried it once, but it didn't take," Harris said. "It just takes so damn long to play. Did you ever get hit by a ball?"

"No, but I had a few close calls. It happens more than you would think."

In the third quarter, a storm moved into the Miami metro area and the game was delayed by weather. Thirty minutes later it was still delayed, and Harris and Jimmy started doing shots.

"I can't tell you how much it means to me to be able to watch the games with all you guys," Harris said an hour later when the game was finally set to resume. "I'm drunk, I know, but I just needed to tell you that. I think that's what the NFL is really about. Bringing people together. Friends. Families. Communities. Whole cities rooting and rallying around a team."

"Chicago gets so amped when the Bears are good," Jimmy said. "My grandpa has been a season ticket holder for over twenty-five years, the tickets passed down by my great-grandpa. He used to take my dad as a kid when they played at Wrigley Field."

"That's awesome. To being Bears fans."

"Bear Down, Chicago Bears," Jimmy said, and they did another shot. "And to the Bears finally winning a game yesterday."

"To the pride and joy of Illinois and the Bears finally winning," Harris said. The game started again. "I don't mean to get all wishy-washy. I'm drunk. I was just thinking about Nick's claim that football is a grand waste of time. That's what he said. Grand. And I just appreciate the heck out of hanging out with you guys. Having a group. Watching the game."

"It's all good," Jimmy said, shifting in his seat. "I have another crazy golf story. Want to hear it?"

Harris nodded.

"I just found out my golf coach from high school, a real asshole actually, was recently struck by lightning and killed, playing golf."

"No kidding. That probably happens more than we would think as well."

Monday Night Football results Week 14
Miami Dolphins 27 New England Patriots 20

*

Monday night. During football season, this would mean a quiet night at home with a glass of wine. Or a night to catch up with a girlfriend. But tonight, Ashley found that she wasn't looking forward to a night alone on the couch. Her other girlfriends were all busy with kid stuff. And Ally, her coworker that she was staying with for the short term, had to study for a board exam.

She walked in, sat on the couch, and found herself wondering about football. Who was playing? What channel was it on? And where was Nick?

From the start, Ashley didn't really approve of Doug so much as tolerate him when he and Nick lifted weights. There was something about his body language she didn't like: the way he carried himself, the smirk on his face. Doug and Nick still lifted three times a week. At first it was the offseason and there was no football to watch. Then September rolled around, bringing with it the 2016 NFL season.

Ashley knew Nick liked football because of his collection of Chicago Bears clothing and posters, including a vintage Jim McMahon clock displayed prominently in his bedroom. Plus most guys she knew liked football. Still, when she discovered it was going to be an all day, every Sunday kind of deal, she felt blindsided.

"The whole day?" she said.

"Yeah. It's what we do. We Bear Down."

"I mean I can understand one game, maybe even two now and again, but every Sunday and every game? That's crazy."

When Gene, Jimmy, Dave, and Nick's neighbor Harris showed up (in a custom-made Walter Payton jersey), she greeted them all, hoping to make a good impression as the new girlfriend. When Doug arrived at ten thirty a.m. with a bottle of vodka, she instantly downgraded him even lower.

She went along with it for a couple of Sundays. She would join part of it and then be off to do her own thing. Mostly studying. In the second week of the season, the Eagles shellacked the Bears and Cutler hurt his thumb. She noticed Nick's depressed mood.

It came to a head on the third Sunday. "It's not just some brunch," Ashley said. "It's my parents' thirty-fifth wedding anniversary. They want to meet you."

"Sunday is my day to rest up and recharge," he said. He was still working part-time and taking classes at night.

She looked at him and he knew he was beat.

He ended up attending the brunch but sat glued to his phone. She didn't talk to him the rest of the day. But they made up. Ashley relented on Sundays and went out to study, avoiding Nick in the evening as John Fox's Bears went down the toilet with loss after excruciating loss.

That February of 2017, Ashley and Nick took a vacation to Mexico. On the beach at sunset, he proposed, on the anniversary of their first date. Ashley accepted and wore a ring on the flight home.

The weightlifting with Doug continued, but so far during the John Fox era, Doug was only able to coax Nick to a strip club exactly once: for Nick's bachelor party in Scottsdale, Arizona. It was April and the weekend of the NFL draft. The Bears traded up in dramatic fashion to draft Mitch Trubisky, but Nick wasn't awake to see it. He had already passed out.

In June, Ashley and Nick were married in Mexico. That summer, Nick and Doug finished their Special Agent Basic Training. Doug found a job with the ATF in Miami. Ashley helped Nick plan his going away party, which took place in August, three weeks before Fox's third season kicked off, at a golf course in Ramona.

Ashley turned on the television, the channel previously set on a postgame show, the analysts incredulous at the Dolphins' upset of the Patriots. She thought back to when she and Nick had first moved in, once all the boxes were inside and they finally had a sofa to sit on. "What was that?" she had asked Nick at the sound of the first ball hitting the roof.

"I didn't hear anything," Nick had said.

Wednesday, December 13th, 2017

Two days after the Chula Vista debacle, a fire broke out on the Camp Pendleton Marine Memorial Golf Course. It was almost certainly started by some nearby training exercises, but just to be sure, they sent Nick and one other agent out to the scene. It wasn't on the 6th hole, but rather the 16th. It was Wednesday, and the course was closed. The fire crews hadn't seen anyone.

By the time they finished putting out the fire, it was well past sunset. Cool air and mist began to flow in from the nearby ocean, shrouding the December night.

Nick went back to his car and pulled on his coat, a coat he hadn't worn since perhaps May. In his pocket he found two old ticket stubs to a movie he and Ashley had seen on a Saturday night. His headache was mild, tolerable.

She always loved the predictable Hollywood movies, and he was always bored out of his mind. He remembered leaving the theater rolling his eyes. She had laughed at him, and eventually they laughed together at each other. He could laugh at how she loved Hollywood movies. She could laugh at how the movies were indeed dreadfully predictable.

But that dumb movie felt like a million years ago. Before the house burned down. Before it all burned down. He put the faded stubs back in his pockets and walked back toward the sirens in the fog.

Just as Nick started his car, the phone rang. He clicked Accept just as the Bluetooth connected. It was his boss.

"Hi, Nick," Alister said. "I assume nothing from Pendleton?"

"Yeah. Just some military exercises."

"Well, have you checked your email?"

"No. Whaddya got?"

"The fingerprints came back from the water bottles. We know who the Links Lighter is."

"Who is it?"

"It's this golfer that was drilled in the head by a golf ball six weeks ago playing up in North County. San Marcos. A course called Twin Oaks."

Nick felt a tingling numbness start to close in on him.

"After the guy got drilled, his friend took him over to the new hospital in Escondido," Alister said.

Nick, very slowly and deliberately, flashed his laminated ID at the military checkpoint. It was like someone else's arm was moving. He put his ID in the cup holder, watching his arm and hand with interest.

"I guess it was a pretty serious head injury, from what I can tell of the hospital report."

Nick heard himself talking. "Golf balls typically travel over a hundred miles an hour. I recently looked it up. Randomly."

"Yeah, aren't they supposed to yell 'four'? And why four? Why not three or five? Or duck? That would make more sense."

Nick's voice was like an echo, getting further away. "Nothing about golf makes any sense."

"Yeah, hmm. So then in the middle of the night this golfer with the bad head injury up and disappears. Just bolts from the hospital. No one has seen him since. Has a family and everything. He's a science teacher."

Nick pulled onto the Five, and it was like the numbness reached the center of him and dropped very steeply.

"All the authorities have been looking and nothing has turned up in that time," Alister continued, his voice getting further away. "He's been careful. Withdrew all the cash from his checking account the next morning and that's it. He fits the descriptions from the rangers.

And the timing matches up with when the golf course fires started—the first one was that week, up near Temecula. We're pretty sure we're looking for the same person. Gene Santos."

His friend's name was like an abrupt bottom. It was like a jolt that brought him back to the present. Nick felt like he was driving a toy car on a little toy track.

"I know him. He's my friend. We grew up together." His voice sounded impersonal, like it was being filtered through some scrambling device to protect his identity.

"Your *friend?*"

"From the same hometown. Since childhood. Both of us moved out to California around the same time. We watch the Bears games."

"Wow. That's something. I'm so sorry, Nick. I can understand if you want me to pull you from the case."

"No. I need to be the one that gets to him first."

*

Gene was sleeping underneath the Eight overpass. From a nearby light post, a red-tailed hawk swooped down and then back up into the air, rising off into the distance.

"Fare thee well, fare thee well, my feathered friend," Phineas said. "Fly on. Obliquely upward and obliquely backward on your wonderful journey."

Monday, December 18th, 2017

Nick was driving, the very tip of an ice pick grazing his brain. He wanted to try Buddy's, a new sandwich place in Liberty Station, the former Naval Training Center converted to mixed-use development. But he got lost in the one-way streets of the arts district, and the restaurant wasn't where he thought it was. When he entered the name on his phone, it didn't come up. He was just driving around now, irritated with the one-way streets. His phone rang as he popped some pills at a red light.

"Hello?"

"Hi, Nick," Ashley said.

"Hi." He felt a lump rise in his throat. There was silence for a long moment. The car behind him honked. He accelerated across the intersection and parked on the side of the road.

"Listen," she said. "We need to talk. Is now a good time?"

The car behind him roared past with a honk and a curse word that went by with a slight Doppler effect. He found his voice. "Sure, I'm just lost." He managed to laugh. "I mean like I'm actually lost. I don't know where I am. I was looking for this sandwich shop called Buddy's, but I can't find it. I'm all turned around."

"Oh, good. I mean, not good. You know what I mean."

He had another call. It was his boss.

"Ashley, my boss is calling. I have to take this."

"OK, I understand. I'm heading back to work anyway. Give me a call tonight. I'm sorry I haven't called you since leaving. I'm in a better place now."

"Me too," Nick said. "I have an appointment with my neurologist next week."

"Good," Ashley said. "I'm glad. Talk to you tonight."

"Ashley?"

"The baby's OK. I think everything is going to be OK. Call me."

"I will."

Nick felt a surge from deep inside as he clicked over to the other call.

"Nick. A helicopter spotted a man with a golf bag walking along a creek in North County. We think it's our guy. We're putting people at every course within twenty miles. We need you at St. Mark's in San Marcos, ASAP."

"I'll be there."

*

Rosie O'Grady's Pub
Monday Night Football Week 15
Atlanta Falcons vs. Tampa Bay Buccaneers

Dave walked in. Jimmy and Harris were already at the bar, in their usual seats. Dave sat down in his spot. The bar was mostly empty. A young family was eating an early dinner and an old couple sat over their drinks in a booth.

"Meaningless victories," Jimmy said. "They would be utterly meaningless."

"That's where you're wrong," Harris said. "I couldn't disagree more."

"What are you two bums arguing over?" Dave asked. Betsy came over, and he ordered a Coors Light.

"Jimmy thinks the Bears should lose their last two games of the year in order to get a better draft pick," Harris said.

"These games don't mean anything," Jimmy said. "If they lose, they get a better pick and have a better team when the games mean something again. Next year. They need to build around Trubisky."

"If they win these last two, they can finish at 6–10 and have some momentum going into next year," Harris said. "Plus, it will give Trubisky confidence."

"You're both wrong," Dave said. "They should try to tie."

"Tie? What on earth for?"

"It's the most humane thing they could do," Dave said. "Losing costs people their jobs. These are real people and real lives. Where's your humanity?"

"You're nuts. And I'm right," Jimmy said, standing. "They should lose. And maybe everyone in this bar—and this country, for that matter—should do the right thing and stop sitting around week after week watching these fellow human beings hurt themselves. I don't know, we could do something productive with our time? Pick up garbage. Plant trees. Feed homeless people. Now I'm going to go to the bathroom before this conversation makes me any dumber."

"See if you can find your shriveled up humanity while you're in there," Dave said to Jimmy's back, which was briefly accompanied by a raised middle finger.

"Do you know if Jimmy was able to talk to Nick?"

"Not that I'm aware. Jimmy called him, but he's not returning any calls."

"Let's text him again."

*

Nick was sitting in the parking lot of the St. Mark golf course when he got Harris's text.

He surveyed the parking lot before typing his response. He had just finished when the call came over the radio.

"All units. Links Lighter spotted along a creek in San Marcos near the Twin Oaks Golf Course."

Nick started the car. His tires squealed as he pulled away.

*

The Tampa Bay Buccaneers kicked off to the Atlanta Falcons.

"All I need is nine points from Julio Jones," Jimmy said. "Should be a cinch."

ESPN showed a graphic revealing that Jones averaged the highest yards per game versus Tampa Bay as any receiver in football against any other team, all-time.

"That would be ironic if you lost," Harris said.

"That would be."

"That's not irony," Dave said.

"Sure it is," Harris said. "It's the opposite of what you would expect, and it would be damn humorous."

"You guys don't understand irony."

"OK, what's irony?" Jimmy asked.

"Your virginity."

"Dude, I have two kids."

"Exactly."

Their phones vibrated at the same time.

Nick texted: *Guys crazy last month. Been down but pulling out of it. Gene is the Links Lighter. On my way to him now. Will tell you all about it next week at Rosie's.*

*

Gene, accompanied by Phineas and Rod, emerged from the tall grass along the bank of the creek. "Look," Phineas said, indicating the horse tracks. "It's a path for horses too."

They walked along the path and arrived at the Twin Oaks Golf Course at 5:20 p.m. A cool (by Southern California standards) autumn wind blew. They cut under the first tee and walked down along a rocky drainage ditch. The ditch led to a tunnel that served as a waterway. Gene crouched in the shadows of the tunnel and surveyed the course. On the putting green, a young girl, likely in high school, practiced chipping with a coach. Across from her, on the other side, an older man practiced putting. Other than that, the course was empty.

Phineas picked up a jagged chunk of granite. "Geology, now that's a real science. The study of time and pressure." He traced lines along the rock with his fingertip. "A good foreman needs to know how to read rocks. The joints and fissures. Cleavage and fracture. How it will break." He held the rock and his tamping iron at arm's length. "You guys weigh about the same, around thirteen pounds, I reckon."

Gene stepped tentatively out in the open. The sound of a helicopter sent him back into the tunnel. After the helicopter passed, Gene once again emerged, cautiously. He carried only his golf bag; Phineas used his iron like a trekking pole.

"San Francisco. Now that was a nice town," Phineas said as they crept along the rocky waterway. "Great seafood. Culture. Really enjoyed it. Scenery. The bay and the fog. The smell of the ocean. The hills. The Wharf. Union Square. A great American city. What I thought would be my eternal resting site, before that act of civic vandalism. Public health reasons my foot. They just wanted the land. All those graves, uprooted. The city moved 'em. Now I'm resting in, of all places, Colma. Or at least my body is. My skull is of course part of Hawwwvvvaaaaad."

They climbed up the slope leading to the first fairway. At the top, Gene stopped to look around, for all the world seeming like a lost tourist.

"Got a job right away. Didn't we, Rod? No vagrant here. Not looking for any handouts. A little farm out in Santa Clara. Working outdoors. Fresh air. Animals. Harvesting fruits and vegetables. Not a bad life."

Gene closed his eyes and let out a long, deep exhale. He was feeling tired. Not just the worn-out, ready for some shut-eye kind of beat, but the deep-in-the-bones exhaustion, the taut and irritable, emotionally spent, enough-is-enough, put-a-fork-in-me state of mind. He opened his eyes and abruptly headed toward the first green, Phineas trailing him like a caddy following a golfer.

They headed down the fairway. After 30 yards, the girl's coach started yelling something, so Gene broke into a run.

"I told you not to wear that ridiculous suit," he turned back to say. "The coat, the tie, the vest. It attracts attention."

"I'm wearing the clothes of a proper gentleman!" Phineas countered, picking up his pace.

Gene ran past the 1st green and all the way past the green of the 2nd hole, a 500-yard par 5. Finally, he slowed down and ducked behind an enormous sycamore tree. Gene peeped his head out to see if they were being followed. He waited a full minute, glancing occasionally from behind the peeling, mottled trunk.

"They say exercise is good for the brain," Phineas said to Rod with a wink, breathing hard, as they approached.

There was no one. The weight of his golf bag suddenly seemed a burden, so he removed his titanium driver, a spray bottle filled with gasoline, and one last match head–loaded tee. Then he discarded the bag in the bushes between 2 and 3 along a creek. He crouched and listened.

"I don't know about you," Phineas mused to Rod. "But I always get a little philosophical at the end of the day."

He picked up a dead leaf and held it up to the sunlight, examining it.

"Life. Death. What it all means," Phineas said, crumbling the leaf and scattering the pieces with his fingers.

"Of course, Rod, you can't truly know what it's like having a brain," Phineas said, bending down and picking blades of grass. "I suppose, in a way, you are fortunate. But in other ways …" he trailed off, rubbing the grass away. A monarch butterfly fluttered through the air.

"Who is to say what the human brain is capable of?" he asked, as if to the butterfly. Then he held up Rod, like they were speaking face-to-face.

"Can you, Rod, or anyone for that matter, say that the brain has a limit? No. I believe it is limitless. The seat of all human consciousness. Memory. Dreams."

Gene moved from a crouch to a slow walk along the woods on the right side of the 170-yard par 3. They walked through a dried-out creek bed and stayed in the shadows of the trees.

Phineas followed, but then stopped to look at a large spiderweb on a nearby tree. He held Rod up, like a child, to show him the intricate pattern. "Language is innate, like a spider that knows from birth how to spin webs."

Gene started running again. Phineas ruefully left the web and started to trot, trying to catch up with Gene, who was suddenly hoofing it.

Phineas held out Rod and spoke to him quickly, the words matching his pace, the tone like that of a lecturer. "Three pounds. A consistency like soft Jell-O. Yet, think of all it contains: Thought. Knowledge. Intelligence. Imagination. Evolution. Survival. Instincts. Genius. Insanity. Love. Hate."

Phineas stumbled, physically and linguistically, for only a moment. "Infinite capabilities. Humanity, like one great kaleidoscope. The sheer complexity and vastness and sophistication of it all, like the universe itself."

Gene rounded the 3rd green and then accelerated toward the 4th tee, still staying close to the woods along the creek that separated the 4th and 2nd hole from which they had come. On a dime, he slipped into the woods like a shadow and tiptoed his way into the brush. Motionless, he stood listening. Phineas caught him in the dappled light.

"Adaptation," he said, breathing hard. "Perhaps that's what we should discuss. The brain can adapt to any—"

Gene was on the move again. He lightly stepped out of the woods and darted across the par 4 fairway. He dropped to the ground and crawled up to the edge of a sand trap, a perfect vantage point to peer out at the open course ahead. He scanned holes 5, 6, 7, and 8. Nothing but a small flock of mallards on the pond. High in the sky, he saw a red-tailed hawk circling.

Phineas reached him, leaning on Rod while he caught his breath. He followed Gene's gaze.

He pointed Rod like a hunter aiming his gun at the hawk high overhead. "Shakespeare. To die, to sleep. To sleep, perchance to dream," he whispered. "Ay, there's the rub. Click." He pulled the imaginary trigger and then held Rod close to his face. His voice filled with emotion.

"And when the brain is damaged, my dear, dear Rod, my companion, my dear friend, always by my side, you and I know all too well that problems arise, like our friend. No longer Gene."

Gene lifted himself to a crouch and clambered like a quadruped toward a cluster of trees between the 4th green and 5th tee. He moved through the trees surreptitiously and glided to the wall of a rest station.

Phineas walked, leisurely now, to the trees. "Look at him. They'll say he's like an animal. But they don't know what's really going on. He is struggling to make rational decisions and process his emotions. If our thoughts are the sea that we all float in, then his is far from tranquil. It is thrashing."

He arrived next to Gene, who was standing rigid on the wall, poking his head around the corner. Gene was softly humming the Johnny Cash song "Ring of Fire."

*

Nick jogged along the 500-yard 2nd hole. The ice pick was still there, but it was dull. In the woods by the green, he saw the blue golf bag. He trotted over, opened the pack on his waist, and pulled out a glove and a Ziploc bag. With a gloved hand he started going through the pockets. In the second one he found tees, a bag of match heads like the ones they had found at courses in Escondido and Salt Creek, and an empty hot glue gun. Silly that so much damage could come from such objects. But no more. The fires would stop now.

He put the tee in the Ziploc bag for forensics and tucked the bag into his pack. He opened the next zipper of the golf bag and found empty film canisters. He thought of pocketing these as well, but the clock in his mind was ticking and the voice in his head was saying, Get moving! Find Gene! Then he saw one of those tools for drawing a straight line on a golf ball with the intention of straighter putts. Next to it was a Sharpie. Suddenly he was in the seventh grade again, at a sleepover at his friend Adi's house, writing D-O-R-K on Adi's forehead while he slept. He knew he had to get moving, but he couldn't resist. He removed the cap and smelled it, remembering the feel of the felt tip on skin and skull. In his mind he was laughing again as Adi woke up in a bright patch of morning sun, clueless as to why the whole group was in hysterics, before making a dash to the bathroom.

Get moving, find Gene! The voice in his head shouted at him.

Nick heard a helicopter in the distance. On the other side of the hole, he saw two agents running, staying low. Random, he thought, that I would think of that. Then he picked up his walkie-talkie.

"Found a golf bag near the 2nd tee. Positive ID on Links Lighter tees."

He kept moving steadily along the creek in between holes 2 and 4. His phone beeped. He looked at the GPS tracker. They had visual confirmation of the suspect. A standard method of pursuit and engagement had been ordered. He was in the second ring of law enforcement, closing in.

*

Gene Santos, the man known as the Links Lighter, stepped cautiously out onto the tee of the 5th hole. Still no one. He was whistling the trumpet part of "Ring of Fire" when a noise behind him made him jump—a loud metallic clatter and the sound of splashing water. He turned to see the mallards fly off. Phineas had fallen sideways into the pond along the tee. His body was in the shallow water and his head lay in the soft mud. The tamping iron lay across the cart path.

Gene ambled over as Phineas convulsed. He stood on the edge of the pond, transfixed. His eyes moved from Phineas to the ripples and the lily pads disrupting the circular patterns, then back to Phineas. "He's having a seizure," Gene said aloud, matter-of-factly. He watched Phineas choking in the shallow water, thrashing about, froth flowing from his mouth, teeth gnashing and eyes rolling. The right side of Phineas's body twisted and contorted. Gene took one last look at the surface of the water and turned to move on.

Tonight would be his final performance. The only attendees would be those of the morbid-curiosity type, like someone that would go out of their way to see O.J. Simpson in his seventies, the kind to say that they were there when so-and-so bit the dust. He was a has-been, a novelty of the past.

Gene heard the crack of a stick from the woods. It must be the critics. The people that got paid to come watch him go down in his own flames. They would profit off his demise. Safe in their seats, they never risked anything of their own; these people were the vultures of art and comedy. How easy it must be to descend on the carcass of a true artist, a true comedian that had bared his soul, risked everything for the sake of laughter or art, only to die on a gallows stage, a slow death in front of bored, judging eyes. Well, let them sharpen their beaks and come for a feast.

It doesn't really matter, after all, Gene told himself. If you produce good comedy and it doesn't reach the right audience, it's still good comedy. As the comedian, you've done your part. What do people find funny today? It's a mystery. Maybe people have lost their sense of humor on a grand scale. Maybe people don't have time to laugh—they're too busy. Maybe they've forgotten what laughter, real laughter, feels like. In the gut. All they have is their intellect and their contempt. So maybe there's no point. Still, the show must go on.

Or maybe an audience will understand me once I'm gone, he thought with a shrug as he heard the sound of an approaching helicopter.

Gene Santos reached the 6th tee and stepped out onto his stage, regarding his audience solemnly. He did none of his preshow stretching that had been a hallmark of his recent performances; rather, he was all business. He stuck the tee in the ground and drizzled gasoline into a puddle around it, then made a trail of gas to a nearby bush. He walked to the edge of the tee as if it were an altar on a cliff, looking out over a vast wasteland. A helicopter emerged from behind the nearby hill. "Hahaha!" he shouted. "I know not all that may be coming. Be it what it will, I'll go it laughing."

He dashed back to the center of the stage and seized his club like he was gripping a microphone that contained all his regrets and disappointments. He channeled them directly into his swing. He swung wildly out of his shoes with a flail that pulled his head up. He missed the tee entirely, the clubhead striking the ground alongside it with just enough velocity to create a spark. The spark caught some of the gasoline-soaked, drought-stricken grass blades and, to Gene's surprise, caught on fire.

He turned and saw Phineas running toward him with Rod, shouting.

"Gene! With drainage we can relieve the pressure!"

"Leave me the hell alone!" he shouted back. He picked up his water bottle and reached for a canister of powder in his pocket. The first shot rang out, sailing over his head.

Gene ducked and tossed the remaining gasoline and powder on the flames, watching them rise like a ravenous creature. The flames were dancing before his eyes when a flurry of shots came from behind him. Two of them ripped through his lower back and kidneys, then out his stomach.

He dropped to his knees and clenched his stomach in agonizing pain. He felt the blood flowing from what seemed like a million holes, like a piece of swiss cheese, porous, and that this was somehow a long overdue correction—that his whole life he had been contained and now he was free to flow. The pain was also like a liquid, a sea rising within him. It climbed through his chest to his neck, and, just as Phineas reached the tee, the pain reached his throat and it was like drowning. He could see Phineas calling out, but he couldn't hear him. For once, he thought, I can't hear him. Then it was dark.

*

Gene felt grass on his face. He opened his eyes and saw the smoldering blades inches away. He could see now that the flames would not catch, that the fire would only burn a small area of the tee and not reach the thicker grass of the rough surrounding it. This fire would indeed be his last performance and it would fail, as he had known it would. He saw faces being extinguished, one by one.

Gene rolled onto his back and stared up at the sky, holding his stomach, watching the clouds drift above. He closed his eyes and the pain was different now, like a spreading warmth. His eyes blinked open to a familiar face. A good friend. The name was on the tip of his tongue. A coughing fit shook his body; his breathing settled, irregular and heavy. Why couldn't he remember the name of his friend? His mind flashed a memory: they were behind a mirror making faces in a Chinese restaurant. But now the face of his friend was on the wrong side of the mirror. The warmth went away. He now felt like he was freezing and that this cold was really the lethal thing to concentrate on. He closed his eyes and felt the cold deeply.

When he opened them again, Phineas was above him, speaking to him. His lips were moving but Gene couldn't make out the words. Just sounds. Phineas removed his coat and tie and kept speaking. Then he went away.

Gene closed his eyes. His thoughts started spinning like a golf ball rolling, the number on the ball like his mind's eye. Scenes rolled to him in a dizzying round-and-round pattern alternating between the ground and the sky. The sky was the scene he was watching, and the ground was a dark interruption that kept repeating, as his mind's eye rolled smoothly to the dead center of a cup.

The first ball replayed the moment he was struck in the head by the 300-yard shot, exactly six weeks ago. But instead of drilling him in the frontal cortex and knocking him unconscious, this time it sailed right past him, harmless as a blown kiss. And he saw his buddy Dave, with the sun setting on his shoulders; they were laughing about the near miss. Their laughter echoed as the image rolled into the dark.

The next ball rolled slow and smooth and filled Gene with wonder. He was at home with his daughters. They were playing basketball in the driveway. The most stunning and mesmerizing thing about the rolling image was how big his daughters were. They were running and jumping, and he was helping them to shoot a jump shot with the correct fundamentals. The throbbing in his head was now a basketball bouncing on pavement. They were all laughing and smiling. His wife called out to them that dinner was ready, but they begged for a few minutes more and she relented. She rolled her eyes and flashed a *what can you do?* smile in the window. Gene couldn't remember her looking more beautiful. Then the image rolled into the darkness and rattled around in his head.

The next giant ball rolled with increasing speed: He was a science teacher again. The myriad students were saying "Cooooool!" ceaselessly. Eyes bulged into microscopes. Cricket legs. Butterfly wings. Veins of a leaf. Students squeezed water drops on a penny, watching the bubble of surface tension. Their glittering eyes observed iron filings on a paper plate splay into the ellipses of a magnetic field. Endless students and endless experiments in an endless classroom that extended down an endless tunnel. He couldn't get over how young he looked. How happy he seemed. The twinkle in his eye as he moved from student to student, practically skipping. His students kept exclaiming their amazement at the natural world, reverberating inside this tunnel in his head. "Whoa!" "Awesome!" "Wow!" Then this image, too, rattled and rolled into the darkness.

The images and scenes started to roll perversely fast. His daughters growing up. Going to college and getting married. Birthday parties. Graduations. Weddings. His youngest daughter had become a comedian. He watched her effortlessly slaying an audience. Then he was stepping away from teaching. Older but still youthful. Joining Dave on his stand-up comedy tour. An opening act. The faces in the audience laughing politely, amused. Next he was older. Traveling the world with his wife. Becoming a grandparent. A large family vacation in Hawaii. The only thing was that none of these balls seemed to go into the cup. Rather they all lipped out violently and started bumping into each other like some absurd combination of billiards and golf.

All of these balls that couldn't seem to find the darkness blended into one giant ball, a scene that played over and over again: the 300-yard shot striking him in the head. He watched, just as the two interchangeable brothers that had played alongside him and Dave had—an arbitrary witness.

He saw himself falling in slow motion to the ground in a heap, seconds before the ball that had struck him landed on the edge of the green. Now he was rising, looking cartoonish in a bright red, horribly cheap, shiny devil costume. He watched as his grinning cartoon devil self set fire after fire after fire, swinging his cheap plastic pitchfork and unleashing hellish roaring flames that devoured whole golf course communities. He was dancing in the flames as the golf courses of the world burned. The last thing he saw, before this final enormous ball rolled over the edge, was the tip of an iron bar extending, reaching in and lifting the cartoonish grinning devil mask, revealing an expression of infinite sorrow and woe. Then there was no more pain. Just darkness.

AN ACKNOWLEDGMENT: YOU AND YOUR RED BREEZER

You are the reader. You are wonderful and kind. Thank you for spending this time with, well, the author. The author is not me—well, it is me, and it *isn't*. I am the narrator. It's one of the perks, as they say, of being in the biz. You get to be other people, do other things, mess around with point of view, make things happen and then see what happens to the other people you pretend to be. It's a game.

So here we go. You're the reader and I'm the narrator, and we're going take this little journey together. It won't take long. It's like a ride at Disneyland. There will be (hopefully) some twists and surprises and things along the way that make you smile, at least inwardly, and overall feel better about yourself or the world or life in general. There might be some slow parts, like the—ahem,— beginning, or maybe you will find certain aspects of the ride that don't really do it for you. But at least you won't have a song like "It's a Small World" stuck in your head for the next five hours. And hey, there's are no lines in the hot sun with your kids complaining about a stomachache from eating cotton candy!

You're a golfer, which I figure is a safe assumption if you just finished reading a book called *Nine Over Par*, but even if you aren't that into golf, you are now, in this story. Because that's part of the rules. I get to make you like golf. In fact, while I'm at it, you're a golf maniac. You can't play enough golf. You take golf trips around the world and spend money on golf when you know that you could probably spend that money in better ways, like wildlife conservation (for the habitats that golf courses destroy), food banks, or Doctors Without Borders. But you're addicted, so you spend your time and money on golf. You have belts that you wear specifically for golf. Your whole life is predicated upon—

Wait, too much backstory. That's the calling card of a real amateur, so let's get into the present. First, we need a setting. How about … a golf course! You're on the fairway of the 3rd hole of your local municipal course. It's a par 5, and you blast your drive right down the pipe. Or, as you like to say to your golf buddies with an exaggerated Italian accent, "the peep lean-eh" (fake Italian for pipeline).

It's a nice day. Warm, but not too warm. Sunny, but with a few clouds. You're feeling good. Let's say you've had a cocktail and you've got that early buzz when you can still concentrate quite well on what you're doing, which in this case is playing golf.

You're thinking of going for the green in two. It's a long shot, but hey, if you really get a hold of it, you can make it. Let's call it 240 out, downhill, with a slight breeze behind you, so if you hit your three wood on the button, and get a good roll, you can reach it. But since you're going to have to swing fast and hard, you'd better take off a layer. And let's say that layer is a breezer, how about bright red, the style of many a college athletic coach. Like I said, it's warm, but not too warm.

You step up to the ball. This is it. Your moment. It's great to be alive, in the present tense. You adjust your visor, your sunglasses, your glove. It's a brand new ball and it's sitting up nicely in the soft, green fairway. You concentrate on your breath, take a few practice swings. Line up your feet. You picture the shot, rolling up to the red flag swaying lightly in the breeze, setting you up nicely for a five-foot putt, your third-ever eagle.

You take the club back, and then it happens. This dude Andy, whom you met three holes ago, somehow lets the cart roll backward so that it beeps. It's a loud and obnoxious BEEEEP BEEEP BEEEEP. It totally messes up your tempo and you top the ball. You turn around and glare at Andy, since he's also talked during your backswing on your approach on 2 and stepped in your lie on 1.

He smiles at you. He's smoking a big cigar and drinking a Miller Lite. "Oh, sorry," he says. "My bad. Why don't you hit another one?"

Why don't I hit that cigar out of your mouth? you think. "No," you say. "No biggie." Because you're not that kind of golfer. You're mentally strong, but you learn from these moments that you need to be stronger. More focused. Less vulnerable to distractions from people like Andy.

You get back in the cart. Your buddy, your playing partner, gives you a sympathetic look and a shake of the head. "And it's only the 3rd hole," they say. (You can make your partner whomever you want. See, I'm not a control freak.)

You drive off, but misfortune strikes. The plot thickens. Your breezer falls off the back of the cart. No one sees it fall. Certainly not Andy and his cigar. You drive off and make par and enjoy the rest of the nine. In fact, why not? How about you catch fire and break 40.

On the back nine, you cool off. Literally and metaphorically (another writer thing). You ride the bogey bus. You get tired. You three-putt here, duff one there, hit one OB there. It gets ugly. You're still having fun, but it's one of those rounds. You had the 38 and, though you're on the 15th hole, it might as well be time to grab a sandwich and go home. You're tired, after all, from doing all the right things and living your life the right way—other than the golf addiction. Plus the setting sun is now behind clouds, the wind's picked up, and it's getting downright cold.

Your breezer. It's not in the basket. Then you remember the 3rd hole. The third shot on the 3rd hole. When you topped it because of dude Andy's cart beep. Well, shit.

You tell your partner all about it. Your partner asks if you want to take the cart, drive back, and suggests that it's probably in the clubhouse. You weigh your options. You could drive back to the 3rd hole; it might be there, but more likely than not someone picked it up and dropped it off in the clubhouse. It is, after all, bright red. It would be a hassle to drive around, on some goose chase, all for your red breezer that, to be honest, has gotten a little snug in recent years.

"No," you say. "I'm sure it's in the clubhouse. Let's finish the last three holes." You shiver and notice the goose bumps. A gust of wind cuts through you.

You finish the last three, telling yourself that you're not cold. That you can rise above the cold with the strength of your mind. You concentrate on the game. But the cold is really getting to you. Andy has a nice fuzzy fleece and says, in his nails-on-a-chalkboard voice, "You've got to be freezing."

You finish bogey, bogey, double. You shake Andy's hand and Andy's partner's hand. (A player about as vanilla as it gets in life, just bland and bland and bland. This character has so little personality that that aspect, the lack of personality, is their defining trait. You can fill in the rest, if you're up to it.)

You drive to the clubhouse. And … the breezer isn't there. You walk out. It's dark. The last few groups are rushing to finish in the twilight. You shrug at your partner, who gives another sympathetic shake of the head. That breezer has been part of your look, your game, your golfing identity, for years. There are framed pictures of you wearing it. You had it on for one of your two eagles.

You ask the ranger, a tired old guy who just wants to go home. There's a moment of confusion stemming from the term "breezer," which is not a part of the old guy's lexicon.

"Like a sweatshirt," you say. "Bright red."

"Nope, haven't seen it," the old guy says with an accent that might be Texan.

So you take the cart. "Mind if I drive out there," you say, "and take a look around?"

The old guy has a push-broom mustache. He fiddles with it, chews on his cheek. It's almost sundown. It's cold. He wants to go home.

"You say you lost it on the 3rd hole? In the fairway?" he says, twisting the end of his 'stache. "Well, I just done drove by there and didn't see nothing. Likely someone behind you picked it up?"

There's a moment where the two of you are blinking at each other. The world is turning. Wars are being fought. All across the globe, there is life and death. People are being born, dying, falling in and out of love, laughing, hurting, feeling alone and together; waves are crashing on distant beaches, poets are sitting on stones scribbling on pages; employees of grocery stores are pushing trains of shopping carts that rattle across pavement; it's mundane and it's beautiful and it's everywhere always happening now and now and now. And it's this precise moment that two humans stand unsure of what to do about a missing red breezer.

"Go on out," the ranger says, "if you like. But we're about to close up."

"Great," you respond. "Thanks."

And that's what you do. You drive off toward the back nine, thinking someone has to have picked it up. It was in the fairway. It's bright red, the color of blood when it splatters out full of oxygen.

Two groups on 18, the closing par 5, haven't seen it. There's a group on 17, the par 3 over the water. You wait for them to putt and then you ask.

"A breezer?" One of them asks.

But the other knows. "It's like a jacket," she says. "Or a sweater. A lot of college coaches wear them."

You start to feel low. It's almost completely dark. You're thinking you've lost your breezer, but something else slips away. It's hard to say what this feeling inside you is, but luckily your trusty narrator is here to help you. You've lost a little bit of hope. In yourself and in life and in the world. You extrapolate from the lost breezer: You're a person who loses things, who is at times careless and easily distracted by loudmouths like Andy. You spend your time playing golf when there are things you should be doing, people you should be helping, dreams you should be pursuing. Right behind this little ball of hope tumbles your sense of meaning. You're out here driving around in the darkness. Your friend has gone home. Your family is waiting for you, and what's the point of all of it, really?

And that's when you see, coming around the corner of the 14th hole, a twosome playing with glow-in-the-dark balls.

You accelerate toward them as they tee off, the balls bright and the trajectories high in the sky that now has stars poking through. There's a crescent moon that you hadn't had time to appreciate before, and right near it, what you think must be a planet appears. Maybe Venus.

You drive toward them. They drive toward you. They're blasting music and singing. The song is familiar. If you had to guess the name of the group, on like a multiple choice test, you might guess Badfinger.

You meet in the fairway. Two guys. Tall, middle-aged white dudes, still in pretty good shape. One of them, though, is quite tall and is wearing your breezer. You do something of a double-take. It is, after all, quite dark. But no, it's clearly your red breezer, and it doesn't really fit him all that well.

"Excuse me, sir," you say. "Did you happen to find that breezer?"

And here, just when you think everything will end with a nice, satisfying, feel-good conclusion that will restore your faith in life and people and the world, this tall dude completely dodges the question.

"Hi," he says. "Fancy meeting you here. My name is Tim Miller. I'm a local author and humorist. I've written two books now—well, five actually in total, but two of them that have golf-themed short stories."

"What?" you ask. "Stories?"

"Yeah," the author begins, approaching you.

His partner stays in the cart. The song goes to the chorus and he takes it up again, harmonizing, like he really knows what he's doing. You don't appreciate this though, as your focus is on the breezer.

"Well," Tim Miller, this local author, says, "the second book is more of a novella, with some flash fiction to fill it out."

You can feel the anger rising in your chest. He's wearing your breezer. An article of clothing that you've owned for over twenty years. You try to take control of the discussion. His partner is really belting it out. An owl swoops through the air, low and soundless. You swallow, try a new tact.

"That's great," you say. "I'm all for literacy and books, but I believe you're wearing my breezer."

Tim Miller, the local author, pays this no heed. Instead he starts thanking people that helped him publish his second set of golf-themed stories.

"Jessica Bell for her amazing cover art. Amie McCracken for her diligent typesetting. Dr. Alka Tripathy-Lang for her profound and thorough developmental edit. Nimmy Dumm for her always careful and strong copy edit. Wanda and the San Marcos gang for their feedback. Rich and the good people at (pause for airplane noise) San Diego Writers, Ink. My friends and golfing buddies for providing the ammunition for these stories. My family."

Tim Miller wants to go on. He can't stop thanking people. Then he stumbles, this writer, struggling to express his gratitude and appreciation to the reader. And that's when you take action. You literally rip the breezer off and drive away. His playing partner doesn't miss a note.

You get to your car and then you realize. It's time to move on from the breezer. That pullover you recently got as a gift, it fits better. It could be a new era, a new you. A fresh start.

VISIT
WWW.TIMMILLERAUTHOR.COM
FOR NEWS AND UPDATES.

www.ingramcontent.com/pod-product-compliance
Lightning Source LLC
Chambersburg PA
CBHW031535310726

48971CB00008B/2493